A MARRYING MAN?

BY
LINDSAY ARMSTRONG

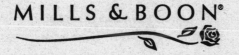

MILLS & BOON®

*First published in Great Britain 1997
Harlequin Mills & Boon Limited,
Eton House, 18-24 Paradise Road, Richmond, Surrey TW9 1SR*

© Lindsay Armstrong 1997

ISBN 0 263 80025 3

*Set in Times Roman 10 on 12 pt.
01-9703-53270 C1*

*Printed and bound in Great Britain
by Mackays of Chatham PLC, Chatham*

CHAPTER ONE

GEORGIA NEWNHAM unlocked her front door, flung her mail down onto her hall table, threw her muddy coat and equally muddy riding boots down in disgust at the terrible weather and walked into her lounge in her socks. Her home was in fact a converted loft above a set of stables, not large but comfortable, with two bedrooms and a lounge separated from the country-style kitchen by a half-wall. It was all wood-panelled in the old-fashioned Queensland colonial manner, but furnished colourfully and luxuriously.

The last thing she had expected to see was an absolute stranger sitting peacefully on her tartan-covered sofa.

'Who on *earth* are you?' she demanded, missing a beat in her long-legged stride, but only one, before walking up to him.

The man stood, and turned out to be very tall—at least six feet four to her five feet ten. He had a thin face, she saw, not handsome but interesting ... a face with a faint scar running from the outer left eyebrow to the temple, hair that was mid-brown, a pair of greeny, gold-flecked, oddly insolent eyes and a rather hard-looking mouth. He wore a tweed sports coat—a very fine, discreet tweed, but not new—with khaki trousers and a checked shirt open at the throat.

'My apologies, Miss Newnham,' he drawled, in a light voice with a decidedly masculine timbre. 'I'm William Brady and—'

5

'I don't care if you're William Shakespeare, Mr Brady,' Georgia broke in angrily. 'How dare you break into my house? If you've come to rob me let me warn you that my father is a barrister, my uncle is a judge and the Attorney-General happens to be my godfather!'

The stranger spoke again and the timbre of his voice struck her once more, and not only that; his cultured accent also held a sort of... what was it? she wondered. A dispassionate sort of irony?

'I haven't come to rob you, Miss Newnham,' he said. 'I'd hardly have stayed to introduce myself if that were the case.' A corner of that well-cut mouth twisted and his hazel gaze slid down her figure leisurely, then came back to her cornflower-blue eyes with a mocking little salute in his own.

As it happened, Georgia was not new to this kind of masculine appreciation, which didn't mean to say that she cared for it—and even less so as she realised that her drenched cotton blouse clearly showed the contours of her bra and breasts beneath it. Extremely shapely contours too, as she'd been given to understand by quite a large body of opinion. But that didn't necessarily commend anything to her either. '*Watch* it, Mr Shakespeare,' she said, through her teeth. 'What *have* you come for? How do you know me when I don't know you from a bar of soap, and how the hell did you get in?'

The last thing she was prepared for was the glint of amusement that came to those hazel eyes, and she said imperiously, 'Now look here—'

'My apologies again,' William Brady murmured. 'We haven't met before, Miss Newnham; all my knowledge of you is from hearsay, but I would imagine it's pretty accurate. As to how I got in—' he produced a brass key from his pocket '—I used this.'

Georgia stared at it. 'But all my keys are silver—' she began.

'Nevertheless, it worked.'

'Well, I don't understand!' She put her hands on her hips and glared at him.

'Perhaps you should take greater care with the keys you distribute, Miss Newnham,' William Brady suggested coolly.

'And perhaps you should take greater care with the things you say, Will,' she flashed back. 'What *are* you implying?'

'That you may have retrieved your silver key from the—er—temporary owner of it, but not before he got it copied. Well, that's one explanation, I guess.'

Georgia flung back her tousled mane of fair hair and opened her mouth, but her uninvited guest pipped her to the post.

'Very effective, Miss Newnham,' he drawled. 'If you stamped your foot, you'd look remarkably similar to a spirited filly with a cream mane—have you one of those in your stable?'

Georgia breathed deeply and decided to change gear. 'If you've come here for any purpose other than to insult me, Mr Shakespeare,' she said, coolly and composedly, 'would you please state your business? If not—don't be offended if I call the police.'

The stranger eyed her narrowly for a long moment, then he said abruptly, 'My business concerns Neil Dettweiler, Miss Newnham.'

Georgia's eyes widened. 'Neil? Oh, now it's *over*, and you can tell him that—from the horse's mouth,' she

added drily, but with the light of battle in her blue eyes.
'I never want to see him again!'

'That's unfortunate, I'm afraid.'

'Why? And what connection do you have with Neil?'
she demanded.

'A—family interest and deep concern at this point in
time, Miss Newnham. You see, he's lying dangerously
ill in a Sydney hospital after a car accident, and he's
asking for you.'

Georgia blinked. 'Asking for me? Why?'

Those hazel eyes mocked her. 'I think we both know
that.'

'No, I don't,' Georgia contradicted him. 'I mean, I'm
sorry to hear he's ill—I wouldn't wish anything drastic
on him—but there's *no* reason why he should be asking
for me. After what I said to him on the last occasion
we met, I'm sure I'm the last person he'd be asking for,
in fact.'

'What did you say to him?' William Brady enquired
evenly, but with an odd little undertone of menace.

'I told him,' Georgia said carefully, 'that he was the
last person on *earth* I would take my clothes off for.'

'Bravo,' William Brady said, then added, 'What a pity
you waited until he was thoroughly enslaved to make
that declaration, though.'

'I didn't and he wasn't.' Georgia frowned. 'There's
something going on here I don't understand. Neil
Dettweiler—who I met at a party, incidentally, and
became fairly friendly with in a casual sort of way—
expressed a desire to paint my portrait, you see, Mr
Brady. He said I didn't have that sort of chocolate-box
prettiness that was so common but something much
more...' She stopped as William Brady quite pointedly

examined her face for chocolate-box prettiness or otherwise.

After a moment during which she was curiously unable to string together any words, he said, 'I see what he means—you've lovely skin, which you've obviously taken good care of, Miss Newnham, despite your occupation, and quite stunning eyes,' he mused. 'But no, not pretty, although well bred, rather patrician, in fact, good bone structure—interesting and quite memorable, I'm sure.'

'*Thank* you.' Georgia subjected him to an extremely arrogant and patrician look from her stunning eyes. 'But, to get back to what I was saying, I agreed, and started to sit for him—which I have to say I found intolerably boring.' She grimaced. 'Be that as it may, he seemed quite sure I was Archibald Prize material, which would be a big coup for him. Only then, when the portrait was about halfway through, he became fixated with the idea that a full-length nude of me would be even more desirable.

'That, Mr Shakespeare,' Georgia said gently, 'was when I made my declaration. Is it all clear to you now?' she added sweetly.

'Perfectly,' he agreed. 'And quite consistent with everything else I've heard about you, Miss Newnham. "A rare old breaker of hearts—not to mention other things," someone described you as. Be *that* as it may, to use your own terminology, and although to my mind I'm not sure what he's done to deserve the likes of you, tomorrow morning you'll be flying down to Sydney with me to Neil's bedside.

'I hope I make myself plain,' he said, coldly and pointedly. 'Because I'd hate to have to indulge in any undignified brawling with you, Miss Newnham—but don't imagine I *wouldn't.*'

Georgia stared into his eyes for a long moment, and was stunned to see how angry and utterly contemptuous they were. It occurred to her that she was trapped in her loft with this well-spoken but angry man, who was not only a lot taller than she was but also possessed a lean, very fit kind of grace and a magnificently wide pair of shoulders... Trapped because there was only one exit and there was no one to call for help.

She said, almost thoughtfully, as the pause stretched, 'Well, I don't know about you, Will, but I'm cold, wet and starving. So you do whatever you like, but I intend to change and make a meal.'

'What a good idea,' William Brady murmured, and accepted with cool amusement the flash of fire that came his way from her eyes before she stalked into her bedroom.

'There we are—reheated cannelloni. But the salad is fresh and the bread is home-made. Would you like wine, beer—whatever?'

Georgia had showered and changed into a fleecy-lined blue tracksuit, and had deliberately and defiantly put on a pair of old sheepskin slippers which she normally didn't parade to the public but did wear on cold evenings at home alone. She'd also tied her hair back, and during all these preparations reviewed with growing chagrin her options for escape, only to decide there were none, for several reasons.

The bedrooms and bathroom in her loft were lit by means of skylights; those same skylights admitted air— but only with the aid of a long pole with a hook on the

end. There were conventional windows in the lounge and
kitchen area, with pretty, flower-studded window-boxes
outside, but William Brady was sitting in the lounge,
and while he wasn't exactly exhibiting the air of someone
guarding all such exits she had no doubt that he was.
He was also sitting beside her desk, upon which resided
her only telephone.

'A glass of wine would be nice,' he observed.

'Please do the honours, then,' Georgia invited politely, and gestured to her small wine rack. She'd set the
table with a red and white checked cloth, matching
napkins and a small bowl of flowers. She'd wrapped the
warmed bread in a snowy napkin and the salad was
colourful, tossed in a zesty dressing of her own making.
She dished up the cannelloni as he chose and opened a
bottle of Beaujolais.

'This is very good,' he murmured after tasting the
cannelloni. 'Did you make it yourself?'

'Indeed I did,' Georgia replied. 'Whatever else men
don't deserve about me, they would have nothing to
object to in my culinary expertise.'

'Point taken, Miss Newnham.'

'Yes, well...' Georgia picked up her wineglass and
studied the ruby depths. 'Should we get *back* to the
point? Your conviction, in other words, that I am the
last of the great seductresses and that I callously *spurned*
Neil Dettweiler. Do go on.'

He glanced at her briefly and continued to eat for a
moment. Then he said, 'Do people call you Blondie,
Miss Newnham?'

'Some do,' she conceded. 'My family, mainly. It's not
a courtesy I extend to a lot of people for the simple reason
that it reminds me of when I was about four, which was

when the name first came into existence. It's something
I've not been able to cure them of calling me on the odd
occasion—my family, I mean. But I tell you what—*you*
are giving me the absolute willies by persisting with Miss
Newnham.'

'Are you inviting *me* to call you Blondie?'

'No,' she said evenly, 'Georgia will do. But what has
this got to do with the price of eggs, Will?'

'Just that Neil wrote to me about you—he used your
nickname, and he's still using it in his delirium.'

'Neil *never* called me Blondie—'

'Perhaps not to your face,' William Brady said mildly.
'But in his letter to me he described you as a blonde
goddess and said he hadn't realised what love was about
until he met you. He mentioned that your background
was impeccable and teeming with judges and
barristers...'

He stopped and raised an ironic eyebrow at her as she
made a disbelieving, inarticulate sound, then went on
remorselessly, 'Then, when I went through his things,
what should I discover but your unfinished portrait?
Whose name should be in his diary, heavily under-
scored, but yours—with one of your doorkeys?'

Georgia, who'd been staring at William Brady wide-
eyed and with her mouth open, closed her mouth with
a click. 'This is...this is... I'm lost for words. No, I'm
not. There's got to be some terrible mistake. Other than
the fact that Neil and I appear to you to have parted,
why have you automatically assumed the blame for it
lies at *my* door? Why, in other words, although you've
never laid eyes on me before, am I such an object of
contempt?' Her eyes challenged him angrily.

He shrugged, fiddled with the stem of his wineglass, and she noticed with the periphery of her mind that he had long fingers and wore a battered old watch on a leather band that had seen better days. 'I made some enquiries.'

'Ah,' Georgia said ironically. 'Do tell me more!'

He lifted his hazel eyes and they met hers with that amusement she'd seen lurking in them before. 'You have to admit you're a colourful character, Georgia,' he said wryly.

'Go on,' she commanded.

'Well...' He sat back. 'Twenty-three, been to all the right schools and finishing schools, mixed in the right society, could ride almost before you could walk, were a show-jumper—those are the kind of things I came up with. Plus the fact that Daddy has never been able to deny you anything, apparently, including this little spread.' He looked around. 'Then there's the reputation you seem to have acquired for being—stuck-up.'

She sat forward and propped her chin on her hands. 'Who told you that?'

'Several people.'

Georgia laughed. 'I wonder if you researched any of my friends? It doesn't sound like it to me.'

He narrowed his eyes. 'You seem to be curiously unmoved by these allegations, Georgia,' he said reflectively.

'I am, mainly because they're untrue, so perhaps I could set the record straight, Will?' She eyed him, then continued without waiting for a reply, 'I did do a bit of show-jumping in my teens, but it was never a career or an ongoing passion with me—just the kind of thing a lot of girls who love horses dabble in for a while.

'And my father didn't buy this place for me. I inherited it from my grandmother, as a matter of fact, but what I inherited was a ramshackle old set of stables on twenty acres of bush, whereas what you see today,' she said proudly, 'is the result of my own efforts.

'Yes, I did borrow from my father for some of the improvements, but I've paid him back every cent and I've turned this place into a successful spelling farm where people know they can send their racehorses between campaigns to rest, be pampered and cared for excellently. In other words I've turned it into a thoroughly good business proposition. I support myself entirely from it and it has the added advantage of being something I love doing.'

'I stand corrected,' William Brady murmured, although he didn't appear to be chastened in the slightest, as he proceeded to demonstrate. 'What about the men you've been associated with?'

'All those men I gave my doorkey to?' Georgia said with genuine amusement in her eyes. 'Don't you believe a word of it, Will! I'm surprised someone didn't tell you how *frigid* and stuck-up I am.'

'So they didn't represent a long line of affairs?'

'Hardly any of them, Will. Hardly any of them,' Georgia said gently, but for some reason a glint of anger was back in her eyes. Although she added lightly enough, 'Nor was Neil Dettweiler in love with me, Will. I really would have known, and taken great pains to avoid it, you see. And do you honestly believe a man in love would want to exhibit his beloved in the *altogether* for the Archibald Prize?' She put her head on one side and scanned him with rueful amusement.

But he laughed back at her. 'It's not such an insult, you know. For a man in love who also happens to be an artist—'

'Possibly not,' Georgia conceded. 'I mean, to want to paint the portrait, but not the exhibiting bit—not the kind of man I would want to be in love with me, at any rate.'

'Then do you have *any* explanation for your name being in his diary, your key amongst his things, for the way he's asking for you?' he asked drily.

Georgia stared at him and felt her skin prickle as she realised that this man simply didn't believe her—and that on certain evidence which *she* simply couldn't explain he was probably within his rights not to. 'No, I can't,' she said baldly at last. 'It's a complete mystery to me.'

'Would it be too difficult to work on the assumption that he hid this grand passion for you *from* you, Georgia?'

'Do you mean . . . ?'

'Yes. Come to Sydney with me tomorrow morning. What have you got to lose?'

'I've got *horses*—'

'Do you have no one to help you with them? For a day or two?'

Georgia tightened her mouth, then looked at him coldly. 'How do I know this isn't some plot?'

'What kind of plot? Oh, come now, Georgia—' William Brady looked at her quizzically '—you're really not my type. I thought you might have sensed that.'

'Easy to say, Mr Shakespeare. Easy to say,' Georgia taunted. 'There's no reason on earth, however, why I should believe a word of what you've said—in fact there are a few good reasons for me not to!'

He pulled a card from his pocket and handed it across the table to her. 'Ring the hospital yourself.'

Georgia stared down at it then rose and walked to the desk. A few minutes later she put the phone down and turned back with a frown to William Brady.

'Well?'

'He's in Intensive Care—they're not making any predictions at the moment,' she said slowly. 'His mother's with him—they offered to let me speak to her.'

'If you wouldn't mind I'll give...his mother a call myself in a moment. In the meantime, will you come?'

'But look,' Georgia said in sudden genuine desperation, 'what am I going to say to him if I *do*?'

William Brady got up, came round the table to her and said with chilling evenness, 'My dear, I have no idea what is going on—if there's a new man in your life or whatever—but would it be such an imposition to ask you to come up with some slight reassurance for a poor guy who is hanging between life and death and *asking* for you?'

'It's no good, I can't sleep like this—look, I've told you I'll come!'

The lights were out, Georgia was in her bed and William Brady was reclining on her tartan sofa, having declined the spare bedroom. It was raining, her bedroom door was open and she'd tossed and turned restlessly for the past hour. 'You don't have to treat me as if you're my jailer,' she added bitterly.

'Count sheep,' he suggested. 'Or fences, triple gates, water jumps—whatever.'

'If you really want me to be wide awake, that's the way to do it, Will,' she said with irony, and reached over to switch on her bedside lamp. In the weak light her bedroom's glory, which had caused him to raise his eyebrows wryly earlier, was somewhat dimmed.

She'd used a mixture of cornflower-blue and ivory to decorate it: ivory carpet and cornflower-blue quilt, stitched and appliquéd with ivory flower-heads—it alone was a work of art. Her dressing table and wardrobe were lovely walnut pieces, there was a padded armchair and matching footstool with a magazine rack beside it, a glorious gold-framed print on the wall, of mountains and snow against a lavender sky, and a bowl of exquisite white roses on the dressing table.

'From an admirer?' William Brady had said on his way to the bathroom, which could only be reached via the bedroom.

'You could say so,' Georgia had replied airily. 'It's nothing to do with you, however.'

He had not replied.

Georgia plumped up her pillows angrily and surveyed her tormentor through the open bedroom door. He'd taken off his jacket and shoes but otherwise remained clothed, and he seemed perfectly comfortable and at home on her sofa beneath one of her spare blankets, with his hands folded behind his head.

Not only comfortable but serene, even, she thought darkly, so that you could almost forget that steely little glint he'd had in his eye when he'd told her the bedroom door would remain open for the night. Not to mention all the other things he'd said to her.

'Tell me about yourself, Will,' she said, arranging herself comfortably with her arms folded on top of her bedclothes. 'What do you do for a living? What kind of women *do* appeal to you—are you married to one, for example? Why do I get the feeling you're a bit of a dry stick who lives in an ivory tower and feels he can afford to throw stones? Those kind of things.'

He chuckled. 'I'm not married, I'm a journalist, I certainly don't live in an ivory tower and I probably like my women a little less flamboyant and a bit more tractable than you. So far as throwing stones goes, I've only relayed to you tonight the things people have told me about you.'

'Flamboyant,' Georgia mused. 'Am I really?'

'Well, you're certainly not a little mouse of a girl. One only needs eyes to see that but I have it on good authority as well.'

'Will, didn't it strike you as being just a teeny bit sneaky—going around behind my back like this? Or are you that kind of journalist?'

'All journalists have their ways and means,' he said, and left it at that.

'Would it interest you to know that I thoroughly despise your ways and means? That I—'

'Now, Georgia, don't work yourself up again,' he advised. 'It really can have no relevance what you think of me, or vice versa.'

'Is that so? What if I did an about-face on the subject of your beloved Neil Dettweiler?'

'Are you contemplating it?'

'No. You must be a very good friend of his, Will,' she said thoughtfully, 'to go to all this trouble.' And she stopped briefly with a frown creasing her forehead. 'What did you mean by a family interest? He never said a word about *you*.'

There was a minute's silence, then he said, 'He happens to be my half-brother. Georgia, we have a very early start tomorrow...' He stopped, and to her surprise she saw him get up and come towards the bedroom.

'Now look here...' she said fiercely, sitting up.

'Calm yourself, my dear Miss Newnham,' he said, with more deadly amusement glinting in his hazel eyes as he came right up to the bed. 'You'd be the last person who was in any danger of being taken against her will by me. But I am going to do this.'

Their eyes locked as he reached for the lamp, and in the moment before he switched it off she read again that cool contempt in his eyes, and for the strangest reason discovered herself feeling young, hotheaded and a nuisance. All of which effectively silenced her as the lamp went off.

She wasn't sure when she drifted off to sleep but it was some time in the middle of some curious thoughts about William Brady—a man who despised her, who was totally unaffected by her, but a man...

She woke to the sound of rain on the roof and the sight of weak morning light coming in and someone bending over her. She said drowsily, 'David...?'

CHAPTER TWO

THERE was a moment's silence. Then a voice said, 'No. It's William Brady.' And the lamp flicked on, waking her completely and plunging her back into the incredible events that had overtaken her.

She said, 'Oh.' And simply lay there while William Brady put a cup of tea on her bedside table.

He straightened and their eyes met. 'Who's David?'

'No one—'

'You mean he's not the reason you gave Neil the old heave-ho?' he queried sardonically.

Georgia flicked her hair back and sat up. 'He is not,' she said crisply. 'Neither is he any of your damn business, Mr Brady, and if you don't want to have to drag me kicking and screaming all the way to Sydney you'd be wise not to say another word on the subject!'

William Brady inspected the luxurious disorder of her hair, the pale, perfect skin of her face, her elegant neck as it disappeared into a fun, hot-pink cotton nightshirt with big white daisies all over it, the imperious set of her mouth and her rather aristocratic nose, and said neutrally, 'Sugar?'

But Georgia subjected him to a scathing scrutiny of her own—the blue shadows on his jaw, the rather weary lines of his face and the way his thick brown hair fell in his eyes—before she said regally, 'One.'

He smiled slightly and spooned the sugar into her cup. 'There you go—stay there; I'll bring you breakfast.'

Georgia regarded his retreating back with utter disdain for a moment then collapsed back onto her pillows with a bemused sigh.

What could you do with a man who insulted you and threatened you, who planned to hijack you, but who brought you breakfast in bed, who, in an oddly laid-back but very adult way, showed his contempt for you but still aroused your curiosity? And made you wonder what he meant by 'less flamboyant and a bit more tractable'—did he really like meek and mild little mice of girls?

She sat up again, shaking her head as if to clear it, and reached for her tea. Five minutes later he reappeared and presented her with perfectly cooked scrambled eggs on toast on a tray. 'Thank you,' she said this time, but with irony, and started to eat.

He sat down on the side of the bed, causing her to raise an eyebrow at him and say, 'Well? What now, Mr Shakespeare?'

'We have a slight complication.'

'Don't tell me—you've decided to believe me?'

'No—'

'Then you've reconsidered and decided that apart from the sheer impropriety of kidnapping a complete stranger against her will—'

'It's not like that,' he broke in.

'Oh, yes, it is, but I said I'd come and come I will, so—what?'

'I rang to check our reservations earlier but the flight has been cancelled, as have all others, on account of a wildcat air traffic controllers' strike. They don't expect to be able to resume normal operations until this afternoon—and that might be an optimistic prediction.

What I plan is to give them a couple of hours' grace and then start to drive down.'

'*Drive* down!'

'It's only a fourteen-hour drive. We could share it but we'd have to take your car.'

'Look, it's *your* brother—'

'Georgia,' he said quietly but dangerously, 'bear with me, please. I thought it might even help you out a bit— to have a couple of extra hours to organise yourself in.'

Georgia stared at him, set her lips, then said, 'How is he?'

'The same.'

'Why didn't you tell me you were half-brothers right from the start?'

He shrugged and watched her dissect a piece of toast with her knife and fork, then lifted his eyes to hers. 'It's a long story, but I guess I thought it might adversely influence your decision if you thought you were also up against *family* disapproval. His family's.'

'Influence my decision?' she marvelled. 'You've blackmailed me, threatened me, insulted me—the only thing you haven't done is allow me to make any sort of decision for myself!'

'You told me a moment ago that you'd said you'd come and you'd come—'

'Oh, look, go away, will you?' Georgia commanded exasperatedly. 'And take the tray with you. I want to get up.'

He stood up and picked up the tray, saying politely, 'Very well, ma'am.' But she knew he was laughing at her.

'And close the door this time,' she added through her teeth.

'With pleasure.'

'I'm going down to organise things with my staff, Mr Shakespeare. Do you want to come? It might give you a better understanding of how well run this spelling farm is and lessen the impression you have that I am a rich, lazy layabout who has had everything handed to her on a platter.'

Georgia stood before him, showered, dressed in jeans and a navy blue sweater, with her hair tied back neatly and her eyes challenging.

'Yes, I would—if you wouldn't mind me having a shower and a shave first.'

'Oh, do make yourself at home,' she said with irony. 'Would you like to borrow one of my razors? They're pink, unfortunately, but they work.'

'Thank you very much, Georgia,' he said gravely, 'but I did bring my own.' He indicated a small, battered grip.

Georgia tossed her hair. 'Come down when you're ready, then, Will!'

Her 'staff' was in fact quite an overstatement, although she was in no mood to acknowledge this. It was she herself who did most of the work involved in caring for the maximum of ten horses she was able to agist in neatly fenced paddocks while they were resting from their racing careers.

The work amounted mainly to feeding them carefully prepared formulas, watching over them as they luxuriated in the freedom of a paddock rather than a stable, and rugging them as the weather dictated. All the same, to do it as conscientiously as she did it was no mean task and she did have one part-time staffer.

Brenda was the daughter of her neighbours, a horse-mad though surprisingly mature seventeen-year-old who was able to combine her love of horses with the earning of some pocket money by helping Georgia out. It was an ideal arrangement since she lived only a paddock away, and, moreover, on the odd occasions when she was left solely in charge she could call upon her father, an ex-jockey, for help if needed.

It was while Georgia was waiting for Brenda to arrive, and as she was making out some lists for her, that she stopped to think irritably, What do I care if he thinks I'm a spoiled little rich girl? Why should I care *what* this perfect stranger thinks of me?

Yet for some reason, she acknowledged, this perfect stranger had somehow contrived to get under her skin. How old was he? she wondered, and decided thirty something. And then she wondered why she should have accused him of being a 'dry stick' yet be unwittingly intrigued by him as a man... As a man? she pondered, and turned at a sound behind her to be confronted by the object of her somewhat mystified musings. It didn't help her state of mind to feel a tinge of colour warm her cheeks.

'Well, Will,' she said tartly, 'what do you think?'

William Brady walked over to the window of her small office and contemplated the view through it. It was pleasantly green and rural and populated by ten alert-looking specimens of the equine world in their pad-docks, awaiting their breakfasts. 'I'm impressed, Georgia,' he murmured. 'Do you have any horses of your own?'

'Two hacks,' she said. 'I still like to ride and I give a weekly class at the local pony club. Otherwise all my energy goes into looking after other people's horses. Do you ride, Mr Brady?'

'Yes.'

'Do you ride well?' She put her lists in a pile and moved round the desk into the adjoining feed-room, where she started energetically to move buckets and feed bins around.

'Well enough, although not nearly so well as you, I'm sure. Allow me,' he added, and helped her to line up some more bins.

'Thanks,' Georgia said briefly, and pushed her sleeves up as she started to mix the feeds. She looked up once to see him watching her with a wry little smile playing about his lips. 'What's amusing you now, Will?' she asked sardonically. 'Or rather, it's obvious *I* am, but in what particular way this time?'

'I was thinking,' he said slowly, 'that you seem to have an enormous amount of energy, Georgia. It actually seems to leap out of you like an electric current—and that alone must be a problem for you sometimes. I mean how to channel it.'

'Ah!' Georgia straightened, winced and pushed a fist into the small of her back. 'So you think I might not be such a rich, lazy layabout after all,' she marvelled, and grimaced. 'Don't expect me to roll on my back and wave my legs in the air, though, will you, Will?'

'It'd be the last thing I'd expect,' he said gravely. 'Have you hurt your back?'

'No.'

'It rather looked like it.'

'Forget about my back,' she said imperiously, and pushed past him to reach for something on a shelf.

'Well, could I be of some assistance?' he asked courteously.

'No, thanks,' she said. 'You need to know what you're doing.'

'I see. When do your staff arrive?'

'She should be here any minute.'

'She?'

'Yes, *she*,' Georgia said, then sighed irritably. 'I only have the one, if you must know.'

'You're in a very prickly mood, even for you, Georgia,' he observed, and she swung on him at close range, opened her mouth to demolish him but suddenly thought better of it as their gazes locked and held.

There was something strangely disturbing about being that close to William Brady, she discovered. Something in his hazel eyes that was both mocking yet amused, something in their proximity that made her feel curiously flustered and hot.

She swallowed, turned away and said crossly, 'I don't enjoy tripping over people when I'm working.'

'My apologies.'

Georgia threw her head back haughtily and was oddly relieved to hear Brenda arriving—although that, unfortunately, was something that would later give her further cause for ire.

She introduced them briefly then asked Brenda to do the horses' water-bins and to take Mr Brady with her to give her a hand. William Brady went compliantly, and with a perfectly sober face, but she knew he was laughing at her inwardly.

Half an hour later Brenda came back on her own with the news that he'd gone upstairs to make a phone call, and said breathlessly, 'Georgie—who *is* he?'

Georgia compressed her lips. 'Someone sent to try the life out of me,' she answered coldly. 'Why?'

'I think he's gorgeous!' Brenda confided.

Georgia's eyebrows shot up. 'Gorgeous!'

'Oh, yes! I mean, he's not exactly handsome but he's so interesting-looking, and he's nice and he's so tall and he...just gives me goosebumps.'

'Brenda...' Georgia had to laugh because of the look of ecstasy on Brenda's face, but she said, although not unkindly, 'He's probably old enough to be your father!'

'I don't think so, but, anyway, I like older men,' Brenda pronounced. 'So...isn't he a friend?'

'He's certainly not, and you probably won't set eyes on him again—so don't dream too much,' Georgia replied with a mixture of irritation and amusement but with a slight softening of her tone because she was very fond of Brenda. 'OK,' she went on, in a more businesslike way, 'as I explained last night when I rang you, I'm not sure how long I'll be gone for—two to three days at the *most*—but I'll ring you every day.'

'I'll look after them, don't you worry,' Brenda said earnestly. 'And I'll water your plants—and Dad's always there if there's a problem. It's lucky it's still school holidays so I can spend most of my time here.'

'Thanks, kid. I don't know what I'd do without you,' Georgia said with a warm smile, and, after a last look round and a few more instructions, took herself upstairs to confront William Brady again.

'Well, Will, what's it to be?'

'I'm afraid we'll have to drive,' he said quietly. 'This strike doesn't look like ending today.'

'*Damn,*' Georgia said, and then, 'Look—is there anything I can say to convince you that you're taking me on a wild-goose chase?'

'No.'

She stared at him, read the determination in his eyes and turned away abruptly. 'All right, I'm all packed. We'll have to unhitch the car from the horse-box. If you'd care to go down and do that—if you're *capable* of doing that—I'll be down in a minute. Have you any objections—not that you'll be able to stop me—if I ring my father and tell him where I'll be?'

'So long as he doesn't make you change your mind, no. All the same, I'll wait while you do it.'

'What do you think I might be tempted to do instead?' she taunted.

'Heaven knows,' he said drily.

Georgia glared at him then picked up the phone. But her father was already in court and unavailable, and all she could do was leave a message with his secretary to the effect that she was going to Sydney with one William Brady, as well as Neil Dettweiler's name and the name of the hospital he was in. 'Satisfied?' she said coldly as she put the phone down.

'Yes. Don't you talk to your mother?'

'Of course I do. I'm just not sure where she is—other than that she's up on the Darling Downs visiting family, of which she has a whole army, and is due home late today or tomorrow. Besides . . .' She paused.

'Go on.'

'Oh, well . . .' She shrugged. 'My mother worries.'

'I see.'

'Then off you go and unhitch the horse-box. I will be down, I promise you.'

'Very well, Miss Newnham.'

When Georgia appeared with her bag, her car, which was in fact a powerful Landcruiser, was waiting at the bottom of the steps with William Brady in the driver's seat.

'Oh, no, you don't,' she said, striding round the driver's door. 'It's my car and I'll drive it.'

He simply shrugged, got out and got in the other side. 'Let me know when you need a break.'

She flung her bag in the back, got in and revved the engine, called goodbye to Brenda and drove off spinning the wheels. The rain had stopped but it was still cloudy and cold. They said nothing to each other as she negotiated the western suburbs of Brisbane and the heavy traffic along Waterworks Road, until finally she gained the South Eastern Freeway.

Then he did say, casually, 'You drive well, Georgia.'

'Thanks.'

'Are we going to drive all the way to Sydney in a stony silence?'

'Why not?' she replied laconically, and switched on the windscreen wipers as the rain started to pour again. She was suddenly moved to add, 'You don't like me, I don't like you—what point is there in idle chit-chat?'

'You seem to like me even less today than you did last night,' he commented.

'I do,' she said baldly.

'Why?'

'Well, I'm sure you don't like me any more today than you did last night for one thing, and for another, taking advantage of little girls and sending them goosebumpy doesn't recommend you to me at all.'

He raised a quizzical eyebrow at her. 'What—do you mean young Brenda?'

'Precisely'

'But I didn't do anything,' he protested mildly. 'I give you my word.'

'Nevertheless, it got done,' Georgia replied—quite irrationally, she realised, but didn't care.

'I'm not quite sure what I can say to that—'

'Don't bother,' she flashed at him, then swore beneath her breath as the traffic slowed to a crawl.

'Georgia, you'll be a nervous wreck if you don't…just let go a bit,' he advised.

'Why should I let go? The last thing I want to be doing is driving to Sydney in this weather, with a man I don't like, on a mission that's not going to do any good, and with my back ki—' She broke off abruptly.

'Ah, I thought your back was killing you—why didn't you say so?' he said exasperatedly. 'Look, pull up at the next lay-by and let me drive, at least.'

She set her mouth stubbornly, then sighed suddenly. 'All right.'

'How did it happen?' he asked a few minutes later, after they'd made the change and were on the road again. 'Your back?'

'I fell off a horse,' Georgia said bleakly. 'It's only a pulled muscle.'

'Did you get straight back on again?'

'As a matter of fact, I did—why?'

'I don't know why, but I was pretty sure you would have.'

'What does that make me? Quite mad on top of everything else you think about me?'

'No. Quite wise—isn't that what one should always do?'

Georgia cast him a narrowed, frustrated glance. 'You didn't make it sound wise at all!'

He smiled faintly. 'The trouble is, I'm valiantly trying to make conversation with you and not getting much help. Uh—let's try another tack. You said you had two hacks?'

Georgia's face softened despite herself. 'Yes, Wendell and Connie. Her name's actually Constancy, and she ... well, we almost grew up together, so I've got a very soft spot for her.'

'What about Wendell?'

Georgia's expression grew indignant and fiery as she said, 'Some people should be shot, you know!'

'How so?'

She moved and settled her back against the improvised cushion they'd made of her coat. 'He was abandoned, apparently, in a paddock with absolutely no feed. He was full of worms, thin as a rake and he'd damaged a tendon in his off-fore. He was quite pitiful when I found him.'

'He looks a picture of health now.'

'He does, doesn't he?' Georgia said contentedly, then grimaced wryly. 'Whilst Connie is like my best friend, Wendell is a bit like my own kid.'

William Brady murmured, 'Well, you've got quite a family, haven't you?'

Georgia's contentment faded and she looked away.

'What have I said now?' he asked.

'Nothing.'

*　*　*

About an hour later, he pulled into a service station, topped up the petrol and disappeared into the shop. He came out with a carton of food and two cups of coffee in plastic cups. They'd passed through the Gold Coast and were winding along the banks of the Tweed river towards Murwillumbah. He drove for a couple more miles then pulled off the road beside a picnic spot with tables and benches. The weather had cleared and it was pleasantly peaceful beside the river, surrounded by the cane-fields.

'We'll have a little break,' he said.

'I should have thought of bringing some food,' Georgia said inconsequentially as she sat on top of one of the tables eating an indifferent ham sandwich—then grimaced.

William Brady contemplated her in silence for a moment, then said, 'You're a strange mixture, Georgia Newnham. A lot more domesticated than one would have imagined.'

Georgia eyed him sceptically. 'I'm sure that's not meant as a compliment, Mr Shakespeare.'

'But it is,' he said idly. 'It's almost easy to picture you with a large family, plenty of horses, of course, organising everything beautifully, cooking up a storm—that kind of thing.'

'Well, it's funny you should say that, Will, but that's how *I* pictured myself once,' Georgia replied breezily.

'What went wrong?'

She'd been looking at the river and swinging her leg, but now she looked down into his eyes, opened her mouth, then changed her mind and said lightly, 'I'm only twenty-three, Will. I could still have it all in front of me, don't you think?'

His gaze held hers and there was something unusually intent in it as he murmured, 'I wonder. Did David give you those roses?'

But Georgia had her defences ready. 'Nope,' she said promptly. 'If you really want to know it was Harvey.'

'Who's he?'

'Who's Harvey? He's a solicitor. He has a tendency to be quite pompous and filled with his own importance and he's laying siege to me in his own inimitable manner—which means to say—' she raised her eyebrows comically '—just won't take no for an answer.'

'I find that hard to believe,' William Brady said after a moment.

'Believe me, if you ever got to meet Harvey you would.'

'No, I mean that you haven't found a way of dampening his pretensions,' he said a shade drily.

'Well…' Georgia swung her leg again and looked into the distance, shading her eyes with her hand. 'To be perfectly honest, he comes in handy sometimes. When one needs an escort one can…' she gestured vaguely '…can handle.'

A faint smile twisted his lips. 'Georgia, you don't. Do you?'

'Don't what?'

'String this man along?'

'No, I *don't*. I keep telling him there's absolutely no future for us. I refuse to allow him to lay a finger on me yet he keeps popping up with dinner invitations, theatre invitations, flowers and so on. He has only himself to blame!'

'How old is he?'

'Thirty-three. How old are you?'

'Thirty-three,' William Brady said wryly. 'And you're right—he's old enough to look out for himself, and if he lets you use him, he does only have himself to blame.'

'Thank you,' Georgia said with considerable irony.

'I imagine David was a different proposition altogether, however. Did you fall for Neil on the rebound from him?'

Georgia jumped off the table. 'You're welcome to imagine what you like,' she retorted. 'But no, I did not, and your persistent interest in my love-life is beginning to annoy me considerably—particularly the insinuation that I'm some sort of scarlet woman. I'm much more like a nun these days, Mr Brady, so put that in your pipe and smoke it. Your concern for the men in my life, the men you *imagine* to be in my life, is— What are you, Will? Some kind of moral rights campaigner?' she said scathingly.

'Dear Georgia,' he observed, 'if you think I've mounted a campaign to rescue every stricken male from your clutches, you needn't worry. You can do your damnedest elsewhere once Neil is strong enough to cope with it.'

'So you don't believe a word I've said—heaven knows why I even bother to talk to you,' she said through her teeth.

'There's no need for us to be completely at loggerheads—'

'There's every need—I could be in danger of bursting a blood vessel,' she answered candidly.

'Why don't you sit down and finish your coffee?' he suggested.

She did, and bitterly contemplated the fact that William Brady succeeded in getting under her skin as few others did.

He watched her quizzically for a moment, then stood up and wandered over to the riverbank where he stood, half turned away from her, obviously lost in thought as he watched the water slide by.

And she found herself watching *him*. Watching and wondering as a breeze lifted his hair and fluttered his shirt but didn't break his concentration. She realised he was a total enigma to her, and, in spite of everything, she was intrigued by that air of self-containment, by the growing awareness—reinforced by Brenda's declaration, no doubt—that all the same he was a dangerously attractive man . . .

'And what is going on behind those beautiful blue eyes now, Georgia?' he said, making her jump.

'I don't know what you mean—nothing!'

'Well, shall we continue on our merry way? Incidentally, I think we'll go inland—through Tabulam, on to Tenterfield and the New England Highway.'

Georgia's eyes widened. 'Why?'

'Weren't you listening to the radio?'

'No, not particularly.'

'There's another severe rain depression around Grafton, and, anyway, the New England is quicker, I think.'

'Oh.'

'Does that mean you approve?'

She shrugged. 'I didn't think I had much choice in the matter.'

He looked at her impassively.

'Don't forget I'm the wicked, scarlet, fallen woman in all this, Will,' she taunted, and tilted her chin at him.

He laughed, touched her chin lightly with his knuckles and said lightly, 'Bravo, Georgia. That's exactly how a wicked woman should look—as if she doesn't give a damn. Ready?'

'As ready as I'll ever be,' Georgia muttered, and stalked towards the car while he stowed their rubbish neatly into the carton then into the garbage bin—which annoyed her all the more, for reasons she was unable to identify.

The road was winding and tortuous as they took the Tabulam turn-off and snaked up the Great Dividing Range. Unfortunately, the rain depression they were trying to avoid on the Pacific Highway seemed to be well entrenched up towards the New England, and at times it was hard to see the road. Georgia resolutely said nothing and they passed through Tenterfield and Glen Innes in what should have been pretty, rolling countryside but was now soaked and desolate.

It was just after Guyra, a little town known for its lamb and potatoes, that another set-back occurred—and a rather terrifying one at that. They came across an accident that must have just happened, involving two semi-trailers that looked to have collided head-on and were now both lying on their sides, completely blocking the wet road, with their loads strewn far and wide.

William Brady swore as a police car with siren blaring and blue light flashing raced past them to draw up precipitately. Georgia stared wide-eyed at the scene of chaos and destruction and said shakily, 'Will . . .'

But he pulled up beside the police car, turned to her and said abruptly, 'Stay here.'

'What are you going to do?'

'See if they need a hand.'

'I—'

'You just do as you're *told*,' he ordered, and swung himself out of the Landcruiser.

She did for a bit, then decided she couldn't stand by and do nothing any longer, for, although one of the drivers was miraculously unhurt, the other was apparently trapped in his cab.

She arrived on the scene to witness an act of extraordinary bravery and strength on the part of William Brady as he crawled into the mangled cab, managed to prise apart with his bare hands the sections that were trapping the driver by his legs long enough for the policemen to pull him out, then retreated swiftly before getting trapped himself.

'You're a bloody hero, mate!' one of the policemen said, and glanced gratefully over his shoulder as an ambulance skidded to a halt beside them. 'If we'd had to wait for the jaws of life he might have lost his legs, by the look of it.'

It was a sentiment the ambulance driver agreed with rather fervently, while the other driver started to shake William by the hand most emotionally.

All of which he bore with a slight grimace until his gaze fell on Georgia, who was staring at him, transfixed. 'I thought I told you to stay put,' he said coolly.

She came out of her daze, set her teeth and stalked back to the Landcruiser.

He joined her a few minutes later, set the vehicle in motion and turned it back the way they'd come.

'Am I allowed to speak?' Georgia enquired.

'Yes, why not?'

'You seem to feel you can order me here, there and everywhere, Will, so I thought I'd check whether you feel your dominance extends to my verbal processes too. Why are we going back the way we came?'

'I should have thought that was fairly obvious,' he drawled. 'The road is blocked.'

'There must be other roads.'

'There are two. One is an unmade road a very long way round and the other is flooded to a depth even a four-wheel drive might have trouble with.'

'I see.'

He flicked her an ironic little look. 'What do you see, Georgia?'

'Nothing,' she said politely. 'It was a figure of speech.'

'Then allow me to enlighten you. They've called for a crane to unblock the highway. It should take a couple of hours at the most. We'll wait here in the meantime.'

Fifteen minutes later, Georgia was standing in the middle of a motel bedroom in Guyra. William Brady was on the phone.

She looked across the room at him expectantly as he put it down.

'There's a slight improvement—he's still critical but stable.'

'I'm glad,' she said quietly, 'but don't forget I was prepared to go the long way round.' She glanced around the neat, very basic but painfully clean little room.

William Brady surveyed her expressionlessly for a long moment then he said drily, 'All the same, why do I get the feeling you've put a jinx on this trip, Georgia?'

She stared at him, then sank down wearily onto the double bed. 'That's ridiculous. All right! I was being bitchy just now, but I resent being treated like a child— and, in case you feel I didn't appreciate how brave you were, I did. But I can't control the weather, air traffic controllers or colliding semi-trailers. And I am here, after all.'

'In person but not in willing spirit,' he murmured, still surveying her. 'And that means we need to talk some more, I think.'

'What about? There's nothing *to* talk about!' she protested angrily. 'Aren't you even a little tired after your Herculean effort out there?'

Their gazes clashed and she bit her lip and coloured because it seemed she couldn't help but compound her bitchiness at the moment, and she didn't like herself particularly for it... 'Oh, hell,' she said abruptly. 'Look, I'm sorry, but you do ask for it sometimes. What *do* you want to talk about, Will? Why don't we make it '"shoes—and ships—and sealing wax—and cabbages and kings" for a change? I might just be able to bear that.'

The faintest glint of amusement lit his eyes briefly, but he said gravely, 'Why don't you get comfortable— or at least get your back comfortable? Would you like a cup of tea?'

She sighed heavily, then, with a defeated gesture, because her back really was sore, pulled off her boots, piled the pillows up behind her and swung her legs onto the bed. 'Go ahead and talk, Will, go ahead,' she invited tiredly.

But he made the tea first. And not until she was sipping it gratefully did he say, 'Neil was a bit of a Samuel Pepys—did you know?'

'No, but I didn't know a lot *about* Neil. So he kept a diary? Bully for him.'

'Yes, although in a thoroughly disorganised, typically Neil manner, and like that other gentleman, not so much to record his appointments but to express his odd, impromptu thoughts.'

'Well?' Georgia drank some more tea.

'Two of his more recent entries were particularly interesting in light of what you revealed this morning. The first one read, "Got disturbed by Harvey Wainwright, of all people. Is the guy for real?" And the other...' He paused and his hazel gaze captured hers in a way Georgia was unable to resist. 'The other read, "There's some mystery to do with David Harper..." And three heavily scored exclamation marks followed.'

Georgia blinked and her mouth fell open. 'Go on...'

'I can't. The entry ended there. Would that be the same David who was on your mind when you woke up this morning?'

'But...but to my knowledge Neil didn't *know* Harvey! And I don't think Harvey would have wanted to know him—he likes his art all framed and preferably old, so he can rely on other people's judgement, and he prefers to ignore any vaguely bohemian effort that may have gone into it.'

William Brady smiled unamusedly. 'It's not Harvey I'm worried about. On the other hand, David Harper is not...unknown to a lot of people—including me.'

'Look,' Georgia said tightly, 'this is as much of a mystery to me as it is to you. In fact I'm beginning to feel as if I've been framed somehow!'

'Why don't you tell me about David Harper—?'

'It has absolutely nothing to *do* with you,' she flashed back. 'Why should I?' But she stopped and ground her teeth as she saw him register the unspoken admission that there was something to tell. Then she said coldly, 'You can go to hell, Mr Brady.'

William Brady didn't reply, but he didn't look greatly disturbed either. In fact it infuriated her to find that not only was he a dangerously attractive man but also, she was beginning to think, a dangerously clever one too, who could toy with her when he chose and then indicate that there was an unbridgeable gap between them—as if they existed on different planes not only physically but morally and mentally as well...

As if I am all the things he thinks I am, she thought. How does he do it? And suddenly it was too much for her.

She leapt off the bed, stifled a groan of pain and snapped, 'I've had enough! Hand over my car keys, Mr Shakespeare; I'm going home.'

'Georgia.' William Brady stood up. 'You—'

'No! I'm not saying any more, I'm *going*, and if you don't let me I'll call the police. You've done nothing but insult me, and play on my finer feelings in between times, and I'm sick to death of it. Hand them over, Will!'

But he didn't do that at all. He stared down at her flashing eyes and working mouth, her imperiously held out hand, and then, before she could believe what was happening to her, pulled her into his arms and lowered his head to kiss her.

'What are you doing?' she demanded, twisting her head away valiantly.

'You could call it an experiment,' he murmured, and added, 'Don't fight me, Georgia.'

Of course she did, but all to no avail. He simply resisted, and then something further snapped within her, as if to say, *All right*, if you won't let me go, you asked for it. And she said through her teeth, 'Well, kiss me, then, Will, if you're so jolly well set on it, and see if I give a damn! Let's just get it over and done with.'

He laughed softly down at her. 'That's my Georgia. I thought you might see it that way.'

What she was quite unprepared for was the way he did it, which was to say that he didn't even commence until she'd stopped breathing heavily from her exertions.

He held her cornflower gaze captive for a while and she wondered warily what was to come, and began to regret her heat-of-the-moment gesture. At the same time she became aware of other things: the faint scar running to his temple, how tall he was and how wide his shoulders were, the warmth of his body on hers, the sudden urge she had to touch her fingertips to the little lines beside his mouth then slide them down his throat...

Things like that and worse—how his hands felt on her body, strong and knowledgeable, as if he knew just how she liked to be held and caressed, knew all her special places, which were suddenly alive and aching for his touch to be repeated, how she would dearly love to kiss this man and make him feel the same way—aroused by her expertise and desirability...

That was when he lowered his mouth to hers at last, and she found herself trying to do just that. With the result that what should have been a 'close your eyes and think of England' response on her part became something quite different—a passionate little encounter of leaping senses and a rather devastatingly intimate and pleasurable experience.

William Brady ended it, however, when he lifted his head, looked into her stunned cornflower eyes and drawled with a wryly lifted eyebrow, 'You'd make a very troublesome nun, Georgia.'

CHAPTER THREE

GEORGIA opened her mouth as his arms relaxed around her, then closed it again because she could not find words contemptuous enough to express her feelings. She went to step away but tripped, and then tried to stand upright, only to find she couldn't, and she clutched her back, this time with a heartfelt groan of pain.

'Georgia?' he said in an entirely different voice. 'Is it your back?'

'Of course it's my back, you blithering idiot,' she retorted with an effort. 'What does it look like?'

'Here, let me help you.' And he picked her up and put her gently down on the bed against the pillows.

She groaned again and bit her lip.

'May I make a suggestion?'

'*What?*'

'Do you think some heat would help?'

'I suppose so,' she said ungraciously.

'Then why don't you have a hot bath? We've got at least an hour and a half to fill. And I'll try and rustle up a hot-water bottle or something for you to take with us.'

She couldn't hide what the thought of soaking in a hot bath did for her, and without further ado he went into the small bathroom and started to run it. He also brought her bag in from the car and helped her across to the bathroom with it when her bath was ready.

'Thanks,' she said briefly at the door.

'Can you manage?'

She glanced up at him and her eyes said it all.

He smiled with some irony but said nothing, and she locked herself into the bathroom.

She soaked for a good half-hour, and when she climbed out her back felt better. She decided to change into something more comfortable and less constricting and put on her blue tracksuit. It was still raining outside and looked cold and miserable.

What greeted her when she left the bathroom came as a bit of a surprise. There appeared to be a minor feast laid out on the Formica-topped table: a cooked chicken, some rolls, a bucket of coleslaw, some cornish pasties, some apples and oranges and a bottle of wine. And there were plates and glasses and utensils from her own picnic hamper, which she'd forgotten was in the car.

'I hope you don't mind.' William Brady rose as she emerged.

'You've been busy shopping, Will!' she commented. 'Why should I mind?'

'I found your hamper in the car.'

'Good work,' she said drily.

'I also got this,' he said, and held up a tube of embrocation. 'In case you didn't have any.'

'Super! I haven't. I suppose you're proposing to rub it all over my back yourself?' she said witheringly.

'It's probably easier for me to do it,' he replied gravely, 'and it might just give you some relief.'

'Now look here, William Shakespeare—'

'Georgia, after the way we kissed each other just now,' he said patiently, 'this would be nothing. You wouldn't even have to undress, just push your top up—why don't you stop behaving like a spoilt child?'

She smiled at him through gritted teeth, hobbled over to the bed, lay down on her front and said, 'Off you go, then, Will, but take one liberty and you're liable to get a black eye this time.'

'There,' he murmured a few minutes later, and pulled her top down modestly. 'How does that feel?'

Georgia opened her eyes. She could still feel his hands gently massaging the cream into her back and had to admit—to herself, that was—that it had been heavenly. 'Better, thanks,' was all she said briskly, and she turned around to sit up.

He put the lid on the tube. 'You've got a couple of spectacular bruises.'

'I thought I might have.'

'Par for the course, I suppose,' he commented.

'Yep!'

'Why don't you stay there? Are you warm enough?'

She gazed at him, then leant back against the pillows. 'Yes, Mum. Thank you, Mum,' she murmured, and looked blandly into his hazel eyes as he handed her a plate of chicken and salad. 'So, Will,' she went on, 'want to tell me why you did it? I really thought I wasn't your type.'

He poured wine into two of her gaily spotted plastic glasses, handed one to her, then sat down at the table and looked meditatively across at her. 'Why I kissed you? It amused me to do it, I guess. Why did you kiss me back, Georgia?'

She nibbled at a chicken leg, then said thoughtfully, 'I can remember thinking at the time that I might as well give back as good as I got. I wasn't getting anywhere doing anything else, now was I?' She took a sip of her wine and gazed at him challengingly.

He said nothing and his expression was enigmatic.

'And I suppose,' she continued, waving the drumstick, 'it amused *me* to think that someone like myself, so fallen and wicked, could tempt you out of your ivory tower, Will. Or at least—well, you can't feel quite so superior now, surely? I mean, we did get a bit carried away together, didn't we?'

He'd been looking down at his plate but he looked up now, and his eyes were bright with irony. 'So we did, Georgia. So we did.'

But Georgia had had half an hour in the bath to deal with the rather stunning response William Brady had drawn from her and how expertly he had kissed her. 'Could it be, Will,' she suggested delicately, 'that your ivory tower was becoming a bit hard to bear?'

'Well, it could, Georgia, I suppose,' he replied. 'Just as it could be that you're not as chaste as you seem to like to make out.'

'Talk about a typically male response!' she said cheerfully. 'On the other hand, who's to say that *my* ivory tower didn't crack a little because *you're* much more of a Lothario than *you* seem to like to make out?'

He grinned. 'Who, indeed? Georgia, I have to congratulate you. If nothing else, you're a fighter of the first order. It still puzzles me why you should be putting up such a fight, and I can't help feeling it has a lot to do with David Harper, but...' He gestured and left it there.

Georgia finished her meal in silence, then said abruptly, 'What kind of a journalist are you?'

'The normal kind.'

'No, I mean are you in television or the print media—
one of those who gets right into the heart of awful wars
or a behind-the-desk kind?'

He pulled a wallet from his pocket and tossed it onto
the bed beside her. 'If you doubt my credentials, my
press card's in there.'

'I didn't...' She stopped and shrugged, and opened
the wallet to find that behind a plastic shield it contained a card with a photo on it which bore mute tes-
timony to the fact that William Spencer Brady was a
foreign correspondent employed by a leading Australian
newspaper.

'I didn't doubt it, actually,' she went on with aplomb.
'So you do report awful wars—perhaps that's why your
reflexes are so honed,' she mused. 'I mean, it was almost
as if crawling into that cab and releasing the driver this
morning was second nature to you. You've probably
dodged a few bullets in your time as well, Will!'

'A few.'

'Brady...' She glanced at the press card again. 'Why
does that ring a bell suddenly? You haven't picked up a
Walkley Award or two by any chance, Will?'

He looked across at her enigmatically. 'One.'

'I might have known.' She grimaced, then frowned.
'Not that I'm that *au fait* with the Walkley Award—
although most people have heard of it, I guess. No, why
your name should ring a bell I just don't know...' Her
gaze sharpened suddenly. 'Hang on. William *Spencer*
Brady! Are you any relation of Judge Spencer Brady of
the High Court? Justice Brady, who died last year?'

William Brady smiled slightly. 'My father.'

'But—but why didn't you *tell* me? He was at my
parents' wedding! I've seen the photos.'

He grimaced and shrugged. 'That doesn't automatically place me above reproach—or does it?' He raised an eyebrow at her.

'No—and you aren't,' Georgia said coolly. 'I just... How did Neil get in on the act?' she said frustratedly. 'He never mentioned a word about being a Brady.'

'He's not. My parents were divorced; my mother remarried and had Neil.'

'Did you go with her?'

William Brady stretched out his long legs. 'No.'

'Why? How old were you?'

'Eight. She actually ran away with another man—Neil's father.'

Georgia's eyes widened. 'How could she?'

'I presume she didn't have much choice,' he said with a wry twist of his lips. 'My father wasn't the right man to try and wrest his son and heir from. In fact my father wasn't the right man for her at all, I think, because she wasn't very tough—not tough enough to cope with him, anyway. He was very intellectual, his profession seemed to mean more to him than anything and he was very righteous.'

'What about you?' she said involuntarily. 'Was he like that with you?'

William Brady said placidly, 'We came to understand each other quite well, my father and I.'

'You mean you became tough too, as he was,' Georgia said, as a statement, not as a question.

His lips twisted. 'That would have been a hard act to follow. And the reason why Neil never mentioned the Brady name—he never does if he can help it—is that my mother managed to instil her bitterness towards my father into him from an early age, particularly after his father left them high and dry when he was only three and she . . . tried to come back.'

'I see,' Georgia said a little blankly.

'And, to make matters worse, during his somewhat wayward youth she had a tendency to hold *me* up to him as a pillar of society.'

'Oh, dear. She doesn't sound very wise, your mother, if you'll forgive me for saying so,' Georgia responded. 'Were you, Will? A pillar of society?'

'Moderately so,' he said modestly.

'Well, how wayward was Neil?'

'Nothing serious, just a general disinclination to study, then a determination to follow in *his* father's footsteps—he was an artist too, but not, I think, with the talent Neil has.'

Georgia thought for a moment. 'But you seem to be pretty good friends now. Why else,' she said with some irony, 'would he write letters to you about blonde goddesses?'

'We are pretty good friends now,' he agreed. 'But it wasn't so much the blonde goddess bit he was flaunting at me.'

Georgia raised an eyebrow. 'I don't understand.'

'It was your esteemed background—crawling with barristers and judges.'

'Now look here—' Georgia stopped and frowned.

And William Brady said, 'Precisely, Georgia. A right shot in the eye, even posthumously, for Chief Justice Spencer Brady—and indeed for anyone bearing the Brady name—for him to marry into a family such as yours.'

Georgia stared at him helplessly, then lifted a hand, rubbed her face wearily and considered that the impossible might have happened. That Neil Dettweiler had fallen in love with her without her knowing it.

'Did you think he would dump you as David Harper would appear to have done, Georgia?' William Brady suggested drily.

She took a breath, gathered some spirit and said tiredly, 'You might as well tell me what you know about David Harper, Will. I really don't appreciate this— underhand approach of yours, you know.'

He paused, drank some wine, then said, 'No more than we all know about him, I guess. Very wealthy, a bronzed, blond Adonis—and a good bit older than you, Georgia,' he said, with a suddenly significant glint in his hazel gaze. 'A lousy reputation with women, if you don't mind me saying so—that kind of thing. Oh, and a crack polo-player—I guess horses had to come into it.'

'Is that all?'

'Yes,' he said slowly, narrowing his eyes.

'Then you're destined to remain in ignorance, friend Will!' she said with decision.

'Are you still in love with him, Georgia?'

'No. I'm not in love with anyone. And I'm only doing *this*—' she gestured to take in the place, the rain, the lot '—because— Oh, hell,' she said hollowly all of a sudden, 'I still can't believe Neil Dettweiler was in love with *me*.'

William Brady put his glass down and said coolly, 'Spare me, Georgia.'

She could have killed him, she discovered. Instead she said, 'Go and find out if the highway's cleared, Will, before I do something I might regret.'

He came back ten minutes later, and if it was possible for William Brady to exhibit the full extent of his emotions he was close to it now, she saw. He looked almost murderous.

'What?' she said. 'It isn't cleared yet?'

He swore. 'The crane they brought up from Armadale has broken down.'

'So, we'll have to go the long way around after all.'

He eyed her sardonically. 'Because of the build-up of traffic they've been diverting it all that way. You know what that means, don't you? Crawling along for goodness knows how many miles on a back road.'

'Well, if you're blaming me for that—' she began.

But he turned away with a look of searing disgust and picked up the phone.

'We're going back to Brisbane?' Georgia said incredulously some minutes later.

'The air traffic controllers have agreed to go back to work first thing tomorrow morning and they're putting on extra flights to cope with the backlog. You don't want to spend the night here in Guyra, do you, Georgia?'

'No! Well, no, but even with extra flights—'

'So long as there are flights I can get on one,' he said definitely. 'Whereas—' his hazel eyes were still smouldering '—this car trip would appear to have been jinxed from the start, and at this rate we'd be lucky to be in Sydney tomorrow night.'

'You are being ridiculous, you know, blaming me for all this,' she said.

But he said, 'Am I?' and stared down at her with his mouth set and such an intense look in his eyes that she took a sudden little breath of fright. 'I don't know about that, but you certainly seem to have jinxed Neil.'

*   *   *

The first part of their drive back to Brisbane was swift and silent. Silent on Georgia's part because it seemed to her that discretion was the better part of valour—she hadn't forgotten that look and she had the distinct feeling that to displease William Brady at the moment would be to court danger.

She did cast him a few veiled glances as they drove along but he gave no indication that he was aware of it—no indication, in fact, that she was anything but an object of utter contempt.

Without consulting her, he took the more direct route via Warwick and Cunningham's Gap, and she'd just calculated, as they ran through Stanthorpe, that three hours at the most would see them back in Brisbane when fate intervened again, causing her to begin to wonder whether it *was* the power of her disapproval that was jinxing this trip...

It was dark and still raining when William pulled into a service station on an otherwise deserted stretch of the highway and asked if he could use the phone to call the hospital. But the news was that their phone was out of order, although they could, they said, direct him to a public phone in a small village only a couple of miles off the highway. It would, they also offered helpfully, be closer than the next available phone *on* the highway.

Georgia watched as he digested this, shrugged and said that they might as well. 'If it puts your mind at rest, I think we should,' she agreed, and received only a dispassionate glance in return for her pains.

However, the couple of miles turned out to be an optimistic prediction—it was at least double that on a series of tortuous, unmade, very wet roads—but they did eventually find the phone and the news was good. Neil

had made some further progress. It was when they tried
to find their way back to the highway that they got lost...

'Well that's good news, Will,' she said brightly.

He shrugged. 'Yes. Do we turn right here or left?'

'I've no idea—I thought you were—'

'But weren't you watching as well? For Pete's sake,
Georgia, in this weather, and—'

'Calm down, Will. I seem to remember that we
came...that way. Turn left.'

'Are you sure?'

'I'm never sure about these things; I've got a lousy
sense of direction and I have constant difficulty with my
left or right hand unless I'm on a horse.'

William Brady swore comprehensively—and turned
right. Three quarters of an hour later they still had not
found the highway. They could have been in deepest,
darkest Africa. They had had a bitter fight about whose
fault it was that was still ongoing...

'If you'd turned left where I *told* you to—'

'Just shut up, Georgia. Don't say another word!'

'You can't order me about like that, William Brady!
I'll say what I like. Do you know what you sound like?
You sound exactly like a husband,' she said scathingly,
quite forgetting her earlier resolution not to provoke him.

'How would you know?' he retorted. 'Or do you have
one of those stashed away as well?'

'No, I don't. But my parents have just these kinds of
fights because—well, mostly because men, it seems to
me, and particularly husbands, hate to admit they're in
the wrong.'

'Of all the ridiculous generalisations, that has to be
the worst. But I'll tell *you* something—whoever the poor

idiot is who ends up as *your* husband has my absolute sympathy, sight unseen.'

'Aha! Now if that isn't a ridiculous generalisation I've yet to hear one, Mr Shakespeare,' she said triumphantly.

Whereupon William Brady tightened his hands on the wheel, swung the car off the road and brought it to a halt.

Georgia glanced at him and said a little warily, 'What now, Will?'

'See this gate?' He pointed to the gate illuminated through the pouring rain by the headlights. 'See the shed beyond? If it's unlocked that's where we'll spend the night, Georgia. Because I intend to travel no further today—not another inch.'

'I see. Will...?' Georgia said tentatively.

'*What?* I don't intend to argue with you either, Georgia,' he warned roughly.

'No, it's not that. I just wanted to tell you that losing your temper like that wasn't such a bad thing.'

He turned to her with amazed irony in his eyes. 'It wasn't?'

'No. It made you quite human—something I was beginning to doubt.'

'This isn't so bad, is it?' Georgia said some time later.

It was a bit hazy inside the old, apparently disused shed, but warm and dry, and the haze came from the fire William Brady had lit on the beaten earth floor. He'd found a bundle of kindling in one corner, and some split logs and a couple of bales of straw, as well as an old car seat upon which Georgia was sitting.

She'd contributed a canvas groundsheet, a travelling rug and a powerful torch, and her picnic basket was open on the groundsheet with their meal laid out: the rest of the chicken and a couple of rolls, the cornish pasties and the other half of the bottle of wine, as well as the fruit.

'Not bad at all,' he said witheringly. 'You've done very well—it must be the managerial streak in you.'

Her lips twitched and she got up carefully and handed him a plate. 'Have something to eat and a glass of wine. I think you might need it.'

'I think I might need my head read,' he replied, but took the plate. He was sitting on one of the bales of straw.

Georgia said nothing, just poured him a glass of wine.

They ate in silence until he looked up at last and across to her, still with a shadow of displeasure in his eyes and lines of weariness beside his mouth. 'You're a model of serenity at the moment, Georgia,' he said. 'Want to tell me why?'

She put her plate down and reached for her wine. 'I haven't had to effect dangerous rescues and be a local hero today, or light campfires, et cetera. And perhaps—' her lips curved into a faint smile '—I have a better developed sense of humour than you, or a more limited capacity for trauma.'

'It's certainly occurred to me that the elements and just about everything else are all on your side, Georgia, but I've mentioned that before,' he said caustically.

'And it doesn't strike you as at all humorous? Oh, well,' she conceded, 'that might be asking a bit much, but what I meant was, I thought my serenity at this moment might be the one small redeeming feature I possessed.

'After all, in the space of just over twenty-four hours you've entered my property illegally, treated me like a prisoner, driven me all over the countryside, questioned my morals, disbelieved everything I've said, kissed me because it *amused* you—which I take to be a purely masculine form of contempt—and now I'm stranded with you who knows where in an old tin shed. I could be having hysterics by now. You're a hard man to please, you know, William Brady!'

'You're sure you're not just gloating at the failure of all my plans, Georgia?' he queried softly.

'Well, to be honest—'

'I thought so.'

'Wouldn't you be gloating? Just a little? Particularly as Neil is making progress.'

He moved his shoulders then slid down from the bale, rested his head against it and stretched his long legs towards the fire.

'William?' she prompted.

'Yes, Georgia, I suppose I would,' he said deliberately, and added moodily, 'What I would really give my eye-teeth for is a cup of coffee.'

'Well, Will, regard me in the nature of providence,' she replied, and, getting up again with a hand to her back, reached for her jacket and emptied the pockets onto the groundsheet. A mixture of coffee packets, tea bags and little sugar sachets fell out.

William Brady sat up and eyed her. 'You pinched them from the motel?'

'Every blessed last one of them—and, before you lecture me on dishonesty, doesn't everyone? I mean, they are there to be used.'

'So they are,' he said wryly. 'There's just one thing— we have nothing to boil any water in.'

'You know, for a foreign correspondent you don't seem to have very well developed survival skills for the small, trivial kinds of things, Mr Shakespeare. There were not one but two Thermos flasks in my picnic hamper, and I filled them with boiling water while you were inspecting the highway. Thus...' she pottered about for a bit, then handed him a steaming cup '...your coffee, sir.'

'Georgia...' He took the cup, and his hazel eyes glinted at her over the rim. 'You're a bloody marvel, and—'

'No, don't say any more, Will,' she teased. 'I could be all undone with too much praise!'

'And I forgot all about a hot-water bottle,' he said ruefully. 'How is your back?'

Georgia sat back on her car seat, carefully avoiding a sticking-out spring. 'It'll do.'

'Would you let me put some more cream on?'

She was silent for a moment then said vaguely, 'Later. You know, it's not going to be that easy to sleep tonight.'

He lay back with a sigh. 'I know,' he said abruptly. 'I'm sorry, I should have thought of that, but I just got— totally frustrated.'

'It doesn't matter. So long,' she added slowly, 'as you don't get to harping again on all my many deficiencies.'

He raised his cup and said with a smile, 'I'm not that much of a bastard.'

Georgia found herself relaxing, and was surprised to realise she'd been tense. 'The one thing I haven't got is a pack of cards. I normally never travel without one, but the last lot got so tatty I threw them away and never got around to getting a new pack. I don't suppose you travel with a pack of cards or a miniature Scrabble set?'

'No, I don't. I'm sorry, Georgia,' he said gravely.

'*Do* you go off and report on impossible wars, Will?'

'Sometimes.'

'Like to talk about it?'

He stirred. 'What do you want to know?'

'If it depresses you.'

'Of course.'

'Why do you do it, then?'

'I don't only do that; I cover some quite positive news too.'

'Do you...?' She paused. 'Do you have a burning desire to reveal the truth of things, then?'

He took his time answering. 'I suppose so. Yes.'

'I can believe that,' she said humorously, then sobered. 'But let's not get back on that tack. Uh... tell me about the women in your life, Will. Has there been anyone serious?'

'Not for a while, no.'

'This is like pulling teeth—was there ever a serious one?'

'There was one,' he said thoughtfully, after an age.

'So why didn't it work?'

He was staring into the fire and she was able to watch him unseen, which she did, with her plastic coffee-cup clasped in both hands and her eyes slightly narrowed.

His hair had dried to a wayward tangle and his clothes, though mostly dry now, were a crumpled mess, yet it occurred to her with an odd little pang that none of it detracted from his beautifully proportioned body as he lounged on the groundsheet with his head resting on one hand. Wide shoulders, narrow hips, long and slim, and she remembered that he always moved precisely and with economy but also with grace. She could just see the faint little line of white that went from his eyebrow to his temple, and felt her fingers tingle as if she were touching it gently...

'Will?' she prompted.

'It... She claimed it wasn't working because I was hardly ever there—although she'd known that was how it would be. She also claimed it would never lead to marriage because I was a touch cynical on the matter.'

'Are you?'

He looked up at her fleetingly, with a faint smile. 'What do you think, Georgia?'

She grimaced. 'How do I know? But didn't you fall in love?'

'Love,' he said slowly. 'Yes, it looked like it at the time. But it was quite amazing how quickly it turned to tears all the time, recriminations. And I suppose,' he said rather drily, 'you imagine I blame her. I don't, and my one consolation is that she has married and seems to be very happy.'

'Are you still carrying a torch for her, Will?'

'No.'

With something like a little inward shiver, Georgia stared down at his averted head and believed him. 'And now?' she said eventually. 'How is it for you now?'

He shrugged.

'Once bitten twice shy kind of thing?' she persisted.

'Such as you and David Harper?' he suggested.

'Not at all,' she replied evenly. 'I mean, what do you plan to do with the rest of your life? Go from one woman to the next?'

'My dear Georgia, I don't—'

'Oh, come on, Will! I may not be your type, and I may be all sorts of unpleasant things in your eyes, but I'm still a woman and, as such, I'd bet my bottom dollar that a lot of girls fall for you. I just wonder what you do about it.'

'You've accused me of living in an ivory tower once or twice.'

'That doesn't mean to say I believe you live entirely like a monk, but I'm sure you're highly selective and very hard to pin down.'

'Georgia,' he said evenly, 'if this is what I think it is, the answer is no.'

'What do you think it is, Will?'

'A fishing expedition—a sending out of feelers. But in your own, inimitable manner...'

A gust of anger stronger than any she'd experienced so far in relation to William Brady overtook her, and she rose smartly and up-ended her coffee-cup over him. Fortunately the coffee had cooled considerably, but he still spluttered, swore, and was on his feet in a flash. He seized her wrist in an iron grip and glared down at her.

They stayed like that for a long, fraught moment, gazing at each other angrily, then he said through his teeth, 'You're a real wildcat, aren't you, Georgia? Is that how you get your men?'

'And if I do?' she retorted. 'What are *you* going to do about it, William Brady? Kiss me as a form of *contempt* again?' She laughed coldly.

'Has anyone taken you to bed as a form of contempt, Georgia?' he drawled, and relaxed his fingers on her wrist, although he didn't release her.

'No one's taken me to bed for nearly three years, Will,' she replied tautly, 'so don't start to get ideas. And don't think I'm fooled by your versions of amusement and contempt—all men are pretty much the same, I guess.'

'Are you simply theorising or speaking from your great knowledge of men, Georgia?' he asked derisively.

A tinge of colour rose to her cheeks, but she didn't evade his gaze by so much as a millimetre. 'It doesn't take much experience to know what men want from women, Will!'

'Or women from men,' he murmured, then dropped her wrist and raked his hand through his hair in a gesture of pure frustration. 'You brought this up, Georgia Newnham, with all your questions—'

'Why shouldn't I be allowed to know a bit more about you?' she objected. 'You've dug around in my life like the Spanish Inquisition!'

'For crying out loud, sit down,' he said with savage impatience, then suggested, 'Why don't we play "I spy", or something like that?'

Georgia said, amazed, 'You're joking, Will!'

'No, I am not. Anything's preferable to this kind of game with you. Look, just do it, before I lose all patience.'

Georgia grimaced, saluted him and said, 'Aye, aye, sir. I believe I may have trampled on some delicate ground—not that you've ever shown the least consideration for *my* delicate ground, which you've trampled on like a herd of elephants, but—'

'*Georgia!*' he said dangerously.

'I'm sitting, Will, I'm sitting,' she said hastily, but in fact had only got halfway down when her back locked. She gasped, paled, then set her teeth and tried to straighten, but couldn't.

'Georgia?'

'Will…' she said huskily, and there were sudden beads of cold sweat on her brow. 'Will, I'm in a bit of bother, I'm afraid—sorry.'

He said something like 'You bloody fool' beneath his breath, but he was at her side swiftly and picked her up and sat her down gently on the bale of hay. 'What's happened?' he asked quietly.

'It's locked,' she said helplessly. 'It's probably only a muscle spasm; I've had them before. It'll go, but—' She stopped and wiped a hand across her face, then swallowed.

'Do you feel sick?'

'A bit. It's just the pain—that'll pass too. I've had plenty of experience—'

'Will you shut up, Georgia?' he said, but gently. 'No, don't say another word,' he warned. 'Just do as I tell you.'

By degrees he got her into a position whereby she was half lying over the bale of straw, and then, using her travel rug, which he warmed at the fire, he alternately put on a hot compress and massaged her back with the embrocation. He wouldn't even let her try to straighten out for a good twenty minutes, then he said finally, 'Have a go now.'

She straightened her legs cautiously and said thankfully, 'It's much better. You're a genius, Mr Shakespeare. Thanks.'

He helped her to turn and then stand up, and he held her arm as she took a few steps, saying only, 'OK now?'

'Yes…'

He looked down at her, then brushed a few strands of hair off her face. He smiled—and she thought it was probably the first time it had been genuine—and said lightly, 'You're a brave kid, if an argumentative one at times.'

But for Georgia there was nothing light about it. Her heart turned over in her breast because that smile was like sunlight after rain, and she had the sudden intuition that she could spend the rest of her life wanting to earn it . . .

She swallowed and went to turn away, but he still held her arm and said, 'I'm going to try to make you a bed— why don't you walk up and down for a bit? But stay close to the fire.'

'All right.' So she did, and watched in some amazement as he rummaged in her tool box, found a pair of pliers and clipped the wire binding both bales of straw. Then with his hands he spread the straw, just as she had done herself a thousand times for horses, until it formed a deep, comfortable rectangle beside the fire, and put the groundsheet over it.

Finally he straightened and said wryly, 'Horses do it all the time, don't they? I'm afraid this is a bit dry and old, but it's the best I can come up with.'

She smiled a bit shakily and tried to resume her previous cockiness. 'I take it *all* back, Will. You're not only a genius but you *do* possess survival skills after all. As it happens, I've often spent a night on straw, with a sick horse or something like that.'

'Well, would you like to try it out?' he invited.

Georgia hesitated and looked around. The rain was still drumming on the tin roof of the shed but there was no help for it. 'I just need to pop outside for a moment,' she said ruefully. 'Won't be long.'

'Well, put your waterproof on,' he said prosaically, 'and take the torch. I'll build the fire up in the meantime.'

It was an awkward, uncomfortable excursion out into the night but disaster didn't strike until Georgia, fortunately, had her hand on the door to go back inside. What froze her solid for a moment was a sudden loud squelching, a terrifying black shape looming beside her, a deep, bellowing roar almost in her ear and, in the light of the torch, pink-rimmed, piggy little eyes and tight white curls...

In the next instant she realised it was a Hereford bull and whipped herself inside with a yelp of fright, slamming the door but catching her heel on it. 'Oh, golly gosh,' she whimpered, and fell over.

'What is it?' William Brady demanded, appearing at her side.

'Just keep the door closed!' she yelled, desperately trying to recover some composure, then shuddered just as the whole shed did the same and another roar split the night.

He did, and rammed the bolt home. There was a moment of silence as they both listened tensely, then the squelching came again, and a smaller, rumbling bellow, which seemed to be receding.

Georgia, who didn't realise she had tears streaming down her face and was shaking uncontrollably, said conversationally to William Brady, 'Just about the biggest bull I've ever seen, Will! That's all. Oh, I seem to have cut myself.' She took her hand away from her heel, having removed her boot, and it had blood all over it.

CHAPTER FOUR

'How do you feel now?'

Georgia, swaddled in the travelling rug and sitting on the old car seat, with both boots off and one ankle bound in one of her T-shirts that he'd ripped up, looked across at William Brady and said regally, 'Fine.'

He grimaced and came to squat beside her. 'You don't look it—stopped shaking?'

'I . . . I think so. I do apologise for treating you to such a cowardly display of hysterics—'

'It wasn't exactly hysterics.'

Georgia waved a hand grandly. 'Whatever. I'm not usually such a ninny about bulls and things, although to tell you the truth I've never come quite so close to one before, and the unexpectedness of it kind of got to me, I guess, but—'

'I think you must be feeling better, Georgia,' he said gravely, 'despite how you look. Your eloquence has certainly come back to you.'

'How do I look?' she queried. 'An absolute mess? I believe you.' She ran a hand through her hair. It was damp and the liberal coating of dust it had had on it was now a thin form of drying mud. She looked down at her blue tracksuit, sticking out from the rug, to see that it was splattered with mud and blood. 'Well, it's been one of those days, hasn't it, Will? I'm sure my face is dirty too.'

'It is,' he agreed. 'There's mud, tearstains and a streak of grease, but funnily enough...' he said slowly, then stopped.

'What?' she asked challengingly.

He smiled slightly. 'A lot of character. Do you think your heel has stopped bleeding?'

'Yes.'

'And how does your back feel?'

She considered. 'Curiously, it seems to be the least of my worries at the moment. A thorough fright must have been therapeutic!'

'Then do you think you could get to sleep now?'

Georgia glanced around cautiously. 'What if it comes back? This could be *its* shed—maybe that's why it was in such a rage.'

'The door is closed,' he pointed out.

'For a moment I thought it was going to break its way in!'

'It won't do that, I promise you.'

'All right,' she said at last. 'What will you do?'

'I'll—keep watch,' he said wryly.

So, with his assistance, she lay down on the bed of straw, and he covered her with the rug and pushed the clothes he'd taken from her bag beneath her head as a pillow. 'How's that?'

'Pretty good. Won't you be cold?'

He crossed back over to the old car seat and sprawled out on it. 'Not yet. I'll keep the fire going as long as I can. I'm also fairly used to roughing it, despite your earlier aspersion.'

'I took that back,' Georgia said.

'So you did. Why don't you try to sleep? It's nearly midnight, you know.'

'That late?' She yawned and snuggled under the rug. 'It's amazing how times flies when you're having fun.'

He didn't answer, and she did drop off to sleep for a while, then woke and lay with her cheek on her hand, staring at the dying fire.

'Georgia?' he said quietly after a while.

'Yes, Will?'

'OK?'

'Yes.'

'Can't you sleep?'

'No. How about you?'

He didn't answer directly. 'My bed of straw can't be all I cracked it up to be.'

'It's not that,' she said quietly.

'Tell me.'

Her lips moved in the faintest semblance of a smile but her eyes were suspiciously bright. 'It's nothing.'

He moved. 'Are you—sad about something?'

She blinked rapidly. 'No. It's just a bit eerie here, I suppose. What with the fire going down,' she im-provised. 'Is that the last of the wood?'

'Yes.'

'You must be getting cold. Why don't you wrap a few more things around you?'

'I've got a better idea,' he said quietly, and stood up. And Georgia had not the slightest idea of his intentions until he knelt down beside her and said casually, 'Can you move over a little?'

Her lips parted and she twisted to look up at him. 'Only for comfort and warmth, Georgia,' he said, his gaze very steady.

She swallowed, then said, 'If you say so, Will.'

A few minutes later he was lying behind her, massaging her back rhythmically. Georgia bit her lip, then said, 'Will, I have to tell you that's...the nicest thing that's happened to me all day.'

'I'm glad, Georgia, I'm glad. See if you can go back to sleep.'

She did.

When she awoke it was a different story. She must have turned, and was now gathered in his arms with her cheek resting on his chest, the length of him along her body—and he slept on peacefully.

The fire was out completely but there was faint daylight coming in through the one high window. The air on her face was cold and still, but beneath the blanket it was warm. She breathed jerkily once, then deliberately regulated her breathing so as not to wake him.

She reminded herself that she had known William Brady for less than two days, had real cause to dislike him if not hate him, but she suspected that it made not a blind bit of difference—and that was ten times worse. She'd fallen for the wrong man again. Only *this* man, she thought chaotically, might not turn out to have feet of clay. This man might just never be interested in her...

She tried to stop it happening to her, but nearly three bitter, lonely years, during which she'd berated herself for being such a fool, so easily taken in, and all sorts of other unhappy things rose up to taunt her in a way she couldn't deny. And with a stifled sob she twisted out of William Brady's arms and tried to stand up.

'Georgia?' He came awake instantly and completely, and pulled her back. 'What the hell...?'

'Let me go, Will,' she wept.

'No—what's wrong?'

'*I'm* what's wrong . . . just . . .' She struggled feebly.

'Georgia, look, I'm not letting you go so you might as well calm down and tell me.'

'You wouldn't want to know, Will. I'm sure the weight of my sins is of no interest to you—' She stopped abruptly and gave a little sob of despair.

He gathered her back against him. 'Sins towards Neil?' She laughed a cracked little laugh and tried to move again, but he clamped her against him. 'Tell me.'

'Not Neil,' she said despairingly. 'There was never anything between me and Neil. I don't know *how* I can prove that, but—' She broke off.

'All right,' he said after a moment, and stroked her hair. 'Tell me about David Harper.'

She took a breath, tried to stop herself again, but suddenly it all came tumbling out. 'I was such a fool,' she said miserably. 'My parents tried to tell me but I thought I knew everything.'

'At nineteen—twenty?' he hazarded quietly.

'Just going on twenty,' she whispered. 'But I suppose for a few years I'd thought I was the last word in sophistication. In some ways. In other ways I was unbelievably naïve. I really thought when he—he took up with me that it was going to be wedding bells and kids and horses—all the things you mentioned—eventually.'

'He must be nearly twenty years older than you, Georgia.'

'Fifteen—but he was such fun to be with at first. I suppose I was flattered—I *know* I was. I felt like the queen bee! Flying around the place at the drop of a hat, all the parties . . . And I could *be* myself,' she said miserably. 'The more outrageous I was, the better he liked

it. Unfortunately, *I* came to see it as a bit of a façade—
I'm not really such an outrageous person—but he didn't.'

'Why,' he said slowly, 'is there a mystery surrounding
it all?'

'Do you mean why didn't *you* dig it up when you dug
up all the rest of my history?' she asked, with a return
of some spirit, then sighed. 'When I came to my senses
and broke it off, I also... refused to talk about it to
anyone apart from my parents. It's also nearly three years
ago, and I was just one of many, I guess. Perhaps more
of a flash in the pan than most!'

'Georgia—' he moved them to a more comfortable
position, still with his arms around her, and looked into
her cornflower-blue eyes '—do you still love him?'

'No,' she said, quite definitely.

'You woke up with him on your mind yesterday
morning,' he reminded her yet again, and narrowed his
eyes as a tinge of colour rose in her cheeks.

She opened her mouth to say that things had changed
drastically since yesterday morning, but caught herself
just in time. 'I don't know why I did that,' she said instead, with what she hoped was nonchalance. 'It might
be that I haven't had anyone to... to wake up to since
then. You know what they say about old habits dying
hard, Will?'

'Yes. So why were you in such a state a little while
ago, Georgia?'

The colour deepened, but she sighed and tried to ignore
it. 'There must be something about this shed that sort
of brought it all back,' she mused. 'Or this ungodly hour
of the day. And it has been,' she hastened to add as his
eyes sharpened, 'a rather barren period of my life since
then. It certainly took a bit of getting over—that kind

of thing does, I guess. Don't you ever have those low times, Will?'

'Of course.'

'Plus you *did* rather bring it all back,' she said tartly.

He smiled fleetingly and kissed the tip of her nose.

Georgia closed her eyes, then said a bit shakily, 'Is there any chance that you believe me now, Will? I mean to say, do you really go around kissing, sleeping with and holding girls you actually despise tremendously?'

His expression sobered. 'You're certainly a character, Georgia.'

'What does that mean—in the context of the question?' she challenged.

She thought he sighed, and then, with some exasperation, he said, 'I thought we sorted that kiss out.'

'The other one?' she said with some irony.

'Yes.'

At this close range, and in the growing light, Georgia could see the darker little flecks in his eyes, and the slightly quizzical expression in them, and she bit her lip and took instant refuge in mockery. 'So we did—a salute between two enemies! How could I forget?' she marvelled. 'Well, Will, should we try to get this show on the road again?'

'In a moment,' he said quietly. 'If there's one thing I do believe, it's your anguish to do with David Harper, although I doubt it's all over. But it should be, Georgia. Don't let it go on colouring your life. Not all men are like that. Believe me.' And he drew her tight against him and started to kiss her once more.

I don't believe this, she thought dazedly, but couldn't resist as his mouth moved on hers and her lips parted, and her body started to melt against his beneath the slow caress of his hands under her tracksuit. I don't understand it, I...

'Will...' she said when it was over. 'Why did you do that?'

He released her and sat up, to look down at her enigmatically.

'No—tell me!' she said huskily.

'I suppose to let you know you're very desirable, Georgia. One would have to be a block of wood not to see that.'

'Take courage and go forth again—that kind of thing?' she said, with a bitter irony she couldn't conceal.

'Yes, if you like, Georgia.' He smiled down into her eyes and it made her feel as if her heart was breaking. 'As I am about to take courage and see if I can get us back to Brisbane in one piece—I couldn't have another day like yesterday, just on the law of averages, could I?'

They were halfway home before they said much more to each other, and then only because Georgia had decided to make the effort in case it looked as if she was sulking—or simply devastated.

'A bath, a bath, my kingdom for a *bath*!' she said lightly, and added, 'Talk about a blonde goddess—*if* it ever applied to me, it can't at the moment.'

He looked across at her wryly. 'I know how you feel.'

'Ah, but don't forget you haven't bled liberally all over yourself as well as everything else. You know, *talking* of blonde goddesses,' she went on conversationally, 'you should meet my cousin Laura.'

'Is she like you?'

'Not that much, although she's blonde too—blonder, actually, than I am—but in the goddess stakes she leaves me for dead.'

His lips twisted. 'That's hard to imagine.'

'Well, it's true, Will. Laura is positively—regal. She has this aura, this composure, this . . . dignity that I have never had nor am likely to acquire, and it never cracks. I mean, she never gets into rages or is outrageous and she's always in control—well, until recently anyway,' Georgia mused.

'What's causing her to crack at the moment?'

Georgia grimaced as she contemplated her own reason for 'cracking', which was the knowledge that William Brady was only going along with this conversation to cover the awkwardness that had come between them. But she decided to battle on with Laura's reason.

'Her marriage would appear to be on the rocks. I never did like James Moreton but I thought Laura could handle anything. It seems not, though.' She paused, then shrugged. 'Oh, well, I might as well tell you the whole sad story—if only to pass the time.' She smiled ironically and added, 'Provided you *promise*—'

'Your cousin Laura's secrets are safe with me, Georgia,' he assured her.

'Well, James, it turns out, is of the barefoot, pregnant and tied to the kitchen sink school of thought. Mind you, his would be a very stylish version of it. He's got a lot of money, but . . . well, according to Laura, he's not only wealthy and influential, he's now also very ruthless and jealous and possessive. He made her stop working— she was a model—and I think he actually frightens her now.

'All of which is a bit of a problem for Laura—I mean, to have to admit she might have made a mistake, particularly after Uncle Adrian tried to stop her marrying James Moreton on the grounds that he'd already divorced one wife.

'Anyway, they had a trial separation recently—that's what she called it, but he was overseas at the time—then she went back to him. Under duress, I suspect. And then he took her off to Fiji for a holiday. You know,' Georgia said slowly and with a sudden frown, 'it's a very funny thing...'

'What?' William Brady asked patiently.

'Laura's the only person I've ever given my front-door key to. I mean, I had one cut for her because she stayed with me while she was—during this so-called separation.'

'How long did she stay?'

'A week, but I was away and so was Brenda—Laura took over, as a matter of fact— Will!' She turned to William Brady with her eyes wide and wondering.

'Did your cousin Laura know Neil, Georgia?'

'Yes! Yes, she met him a couple of times when he was painting my portrait!'

'And would it be fair to say that if she fell in love with someone else and was having an affair she wouldn't exactly flaunt it before this James Moreton?'

'Yes!'

'Mum, it's Georgia—how are you? How was Toowoomba? Mum, is Laura back from Fiji? Is she home—with James?'

The first thing she'd done on getting home was grab the phone, all thoughts of baths and everything else having faded from her mind.

'Georgia, darling, where have you been?' her mother demanded down the line. 'Your father got this strange message yesterday morning that he couldn't make head nor tail of! And the weather's been so dreadful!'

'Oh, I've been—uh—fine—'

'But who is this William Brady? We've never heard of him!'

'As a matter of fact you probably have; he's Spencer Brady's son,' Georgia said, flicking a little look at her companion. 'But—'

'Darling!' her mother said delightedly. 'Why didn't you tell me you knew him? Not that I know him, but your father and his father were at university together and he was at our wedding—I'm sure I've shown you the photo. Is it anything serious?'

'Yes, you have, and no, Mum, it's entirely *unserious*,' Georgia replied pointedly. 'But about Laura—'

'Well, why would you rush off with him to Sydney, then?'

Georgia sighed. 'I'll explain some other time, Mum. Please, *is* Laura home?'

'Yes, she got home the day before yesterday. They were lucky they made it before this chaos with the air traffic whoevers, but—'

'Good, then she must be out shopping or something. I'll try her on the phone again. Mum, love you—I'll ring back later.'

'She's coming; she'll be here in half an hour,' Georgia said after her cousin had finally answered her phone.

'What did she say when you mentioned Neil?'

'She was stunned,' Georgia said slowly, then added with extreme exasperation, 'Why couldn't she have confided in me?'

He shrugged. 'I suppose it all hangs on how ruthless James Moreton is.'

'But to use me as a decoy!'

He studied her for a moment, then said quietly, 'Why don't you have that bath, Georgia? Although... would it be too much to ask if I could have a quick shower first?'

'No, of course not. Go ahead,' she said absently.

In the end she didn't have a bath, but they were both showered and changed into clean clothes—William into his one spare set and Georgia into fawn trousers and a chunky cream sweater—before Laura arrived.

'Glory be,' Georgia said in the minutes before her cousin was due as she walked out of her bedroom with her hair still wet and loose. 'I feel like a different person. And you look like one, Will.'

His spare set of clothes comprised a pair of blue jeans and a mulberry jumper. He smiled faintly. 'How's the heel and your back?'

'Both OK, thanks. Look, Will, would you mind if I had a word with Laura first?' Her cornflower gaze was direct and serious. 'There are a couple of things I need to know.'

He hesitated briefly, then nodded, and they both turned at the sound of a car.

'You could wait in the bedroom,' she suggested.

'Georgia!' It was a curiously distraught-looking Laura—pale, shaken and a far cry from her usual *soignée*, glorious, golden self—who greeted her cousin. 'Oh,

Georgie, why didn't you tell me you knew about me and Neil?'

'Come in, Laura. Sit down,' Georgia said a shade drily, and pulled out a chair for her at the kitchen table. She was making tea. 'I didn't, at the time.'

'But on the phone you said was it true about me and Neil! And then not another word!'

'Is it?'

'Oh, *yes*,' Laura said in anguish. 'I didn't believe it could happen to me—not after what I've been through with James. I thought I was immune to ever falling in love again. And that it should be someone like Neil,' she said huskily, 'who lives like a gypsy, who is fanatical about his art to the extent that he even forgets I exist sometimes, who even calls me Blondie... But it is.'

'And you carried on a kind of clandestine affair with Neil right *here*—even had one of my keys made for him— while I was away?'

'I'm sorry,' Laura whispered, 'but I was so afraid of James finding out.'

'Well, what *about* James?' Georgia asked.

'Do you know what I was doing when you rang, Georgie? Packing. I'm leaving him.'

'Would you—? Without Neil, would you have done it?'

'*Yes!*' Laura said with some of her old spirit. 'I made a terrible mistake in marrying him. He virtually forced me to go to Fiji with him, and when we got back I knew I couldn't go on, so I plucked up courage this morning and—told Dad. I should have done it ages ago, because if there's one person who can handle James he can, but—' she gestured wryly '—I also knew he'd say "I *told* you so".'

Georgia thought of her uncle Adrian, who was one of those larger than life people as well as being particularly influential himself, and smiled absently. 'Did he?'

'Yes,' Laura said tremulously. 'He called me all kinds of a fool. But then he said, "There's not a man alive who can get away with mistreating *my* daughter!"'

They laughed together briefly, then Georgia sobered and said, 'Did you tell him about Neil?'

'No.' Laura grimaced. 'I thought one shock at a time might be the way to go—and, anyway, I asked Neil to give me some space so I could sort myself out.'

'I see. Well, there's someone here you should meet, Laura.'

'Meet?' For an instant there was a wild glimmer of hope in Laura's eyes.

'No, it's not Neil,' Georgia said hastily, 'but perhaps the next best thing. You may not have heard of William Shakespeare alias Brady, but he's Neil Dettweiler's half-brother. Will!' she called. 'You can come out now.'

'Shakespeare—Brady?' Laura said bewilderedly.

'Georgia is just having her bit of fun, Laura—may I call you that?' William Brady murmured, coming into the kitchen and holding out his hand.

'Of course—but I still don't understand.' Laura shook William's hand and stared at him.

'Darling,' Georgia said flippantly to her, 'you're lucky your period of not understanding is to be so short! Mine was a lot longer and a lot less comfortable, believe me.' And she shot William Brady a telling blue look. 'By the way, did Harvey disturb you and Neil one day?'

'Harvey? Yes, as a matter of fact. Not that he saw Neil, although Neil heard him—Georgia, he's so pompous, he's unbelievable, but— Oh, I am sorry,' Laura said contritely.

'And did you tell Neil about David Harper?'

'I—' some colour disturbed Laura's cheeks '—I may have, but I didn't give away any secrets. I don't really *know* any. Look, what is this about, anyway?' She stared from one to the other.

'Laura—' William began, but Georgia overrode him.

'Laura, so there can be absolutely no more misunderstandings, did you also caution Neil to be discreet— to the point of not even mentioning your name in his diary?'

'Well...' Laura wrung her hands.

'Even to the point of using *me* as a decoy, in other words?' Georgia persisted.

'Oh—yes,' Laura said miserably. 'But you don't know what James is like, what he might have done! And we couldn't really see the harm in it, Georgie.'

Georgia laughed. 'And couldn't ever know how successful you'd be, probably. Tell her, Will!' She looked challengingly across at him.

'Georgia, I apologise,' William Brady said quietly, holding her gaze in a mysterious little exercise of power. 'Unreservedly.'

'Tell me what?' Laura said.

He looked at her at last. 'Neil has had an accident and he's asking for— Put it this way, I thought the person he was asking for was Georgia.'

'Moreover, William has been trying to take me to Neil's bedside for the last two days,' Georgia said with irony, then stopped as Laura stood up, said something inaudible, went white as a sheet and started to faint.

'Now look what you've done!' Georgia accused William Brady as they both tripped over chairs in their efforts to catch Laura.

'*I've* done?' he retorted. 'Talk about the Spanish Inquisition—I've got her.'

'Well, what are you going to do with her? You can't hold her up like the Statue of Liberty for ever,' Georgia said crossly. 'Bring her into the lounge,' she commanded.

So William Brady picked Laura up and carried her over to the tartan settee, where he set her down carefully, and Georgia sat down beside her and started to massage her hands vigorously, talking all the time.

'It's *all right*, Laura. He—Neil—is making progress, and if William is as good as his word he'll be able to get you both down to Sydney today. Darling, wake up! I appreciate how you must feel but now's not a good time to behave like a wet weekend. You're better than that, and—'

'Here,' William Brady said drily, and put a glass of brandy into Georgia's hand. 'Do you have to be so vigorous—verbally and otherwise?'

Georgia shot him a vigorously angry look, took a sudden mouthful of the brandy herself then put the glass to Laura's pale lips as her lashes fluttered up. And William Brady picked up the phone.

By the time he put it down Laura had regained her senses, although she still looked pale, and she and Georgia turned to him.

'I've managed to get a seat on the three o'clock flight this afternoon—but only one.'

'Oh, please,' Laura said beseechingly, 'can I have it?'

'Well, Will,' Georgia said as they waved Laura off, 'I don't know why you didn't accept her offer of a lift.'

He looked down at her meditatively. 'I've nowhere to go at the moment, Georgia.'

She shrugged. 'You might have got on a later flight.'

'And I might have done my dash with Laura's seat. Conditions are chaotic, according to my source,' he said placidly. 'School holidays end tomorrow.'

'Well, what *do* you intend to do with yourself in the meantime?' Georgia asked exasperatedly.

'I don't know. Any suggestions?'

'No,' she said shortly. 'But I know what I'm going to do—go and see my horses. You please yourself, Will,' she said, with a flip of her hand.

He didn't follow her and she didn't turn back to see what he did do.

There'd been no sign of Brenda when they'd arrived but everything in the stable was spick and span and Wendell and Connie greeted her affectionately.

Georgia checked all the horses in the paddocks and found them to be all in order too, but she spent a bit of time changing their rugs to lighter-weight ones as the sun came out, and it was well into the afternoon before she went upstairs again, wondering as she did so whether she would find William Brady still in residence. Perhaps he took the hint and ordered a taxi while I was out of sight and hearing, she thought.

But he hadn't. In fact he was fast asleep on her settee, and he neither moved nor woke as she stood looking down at him for a long moment. Then she turned away and padded through to her bedroom, closed the door quietly and lay down herself.

CHAPTER FIVE

IT WAS quite dark when she woke, and her bedside clock told her it was seven-thirty. She got up with a stifled exclamation and rushed out of her bedroom—to stop dead at what she saw, heard and smelt.

A lovely herb and wine aroma was what she smelt; she saw that her kitchen table was set for two, that the lamps were on in the lounge, and Mendelssohn was what she heard pouring softly from her compact disc player. She also saw William Brady with a teatowel in his hand in the kitchen.

'What . . . ?' she said dazedly. Then, more coherently, 'The horses! I put light rugs on because it had warmed up a bit, but—'

'Relax, Georgia,' William Brady recommended. 'When Brenda arrived to feed up, I helped her, and we changed rugs et cetera and they're all fine.'

'But . . .'

'And I've taken the liberty of cooking you dinner,' he went on smoothly. 'Why don't you have that bath you were so longing for earlier?' He glanced at his watch. 'You've got about half an hour.'

Georgia ran a hand through her hair, opened her mouth, blinked, then without a word turned on her heel and went back into her bedroom.

She spent twenty minutes soaking in the bath amidst the steamy fragrance of the gardenia bath salts her mother had given her for her birthday, and wondered

what else William Brady had in store for her. Then she
dressed in a pair of navy stretch ski-pants and a long
violet-blue cable sweater, leaving her hair, restored to its
usual shining fairness, loose.

She studied her features in her bathroom mirror for
a time, looking for 'character' but seeing a certain un-
certainty in her eyes that was deeply disturbing. So she
took a steadying breath, pushed up the sleeves of the
sweater, which tended to fall over her hands, and studied
her fingers with their short, unpainted nails.

She cautioned herself against all sorts of things as she
then applied moisturiser to her skin and a touch of lip-
stick to her mouth—for courage? she wondered. And,
with a touch of defiance, she put on her sheepskin
slippers and sallied forth.

Mendelssohn had changed to Mozart, the lovely
Romanza of his D minor Piano Concerto that had
brought the movie *Amadeus* to a close, and she accepted
a glass of wine from William Brady, accepted his brief
but oddly penetrating head-to-toe assessment of her
bathed, tidied and perfumed person, and said the first
thing that came to mind.

'Perhaps it had its flaws—I know some people who
hated its interpretation of Mozart—but the music was
so magnificent I can never hear this without being drawn
right back into his life and times, and wanting to shed
a tear or two.'

He smiled down at her. 'Same with me. I can still see
the rain dripping down, and I still feel bereft.'

Georgia took a stunned little breath—because she
hadn't expected to share an experience like this with him?
Hadn't expected to find a kindred spirit who understood
what she was saying without elaborate explanations? No,

I'm being silly, she told herself. Millions of people were moved by *Amadeus*, I'm sure.

She took a sip of her wine and said, 'I'm a bit of an expert, you know.'

'On Mozart?'

'Yes. I can tell you when he was born, when he died, the names of his dog and his sister, and of his two children who survived—do you know *he* was baptised Johannes Chrysostomus Wolfgangus Theophilus Mozart, commonly known as Wolferl?'

'As a matter of fact I do. I also know that Theophilus is the Greek form of the Latin Amadeus, which he preferred, and that they both mean "beloved of God".'

Georgia grinned at him. 'Perhaps we read the same book.'

'Perhaps. Talking of books—' he picked up one that was lying on her coffee-table '—did you enjoy this?'

'Yes, I did,' Georgia said enthusiastically. 'I don't usually go in for travelogues and politico-social comment at the same time, but it's very funny, *very* acute and I got to know enough about Micronesia, Melanesia and Polynesia—which I have to confess was all a bit blurred for me—to tell the difference now. My father gave it to me for Christmas. He said this B.S. Williams is acquiring quite a formidable reputation. Would you like to borrow it?'

'I've read it, thanks,' he said with a faint smile.

'Well, he *is* good, isn't he?'

'I would like to think so. By the way, dinner is about to be served.'

Dinner was a beef and mushroom casserole accompanied by a dish of potatoes Anna and fresh green beans. It was delicious and delicately seasoned and she couldn't have bettered it herself.

'I grant you this, Will, you're a man of many talents!' She raised her glass to him when she'd finished the last mouthful. 'It's also just as well we came home when we did—I'd forgotten I'd left the fridge full of food.'

'Your kitchen is a pleasure to work in, Georgia,' he replied. 'Plenty of herbs and things.'

'Have you thought you could get a job as a chef if the journalism ever lets you down?'

He grimaced. 'I only cook when the mood takes me.'

'So what took you to it this afternoon? I mean, what induced the mood?'

He raised a wry eyebrow. 'I was starving, for one thing.'

She laughed. 'We did forget a bit about food today, didn't we? Another one of those days. But they're improving—well—' she shrugged '—I hope they are.'

'So is Neil,' he said quietly.

Georgia put a hand to her mouth and said contritely, 'I forgot to ask—I'm glad. Did you ring recently?'

'Yes—Laura arrived safely, is installed at his side, and the effect has been pretty beneficial, apparently. They expect him to be out of Intensive Care tomorrow but it will be at least a fortnight before he leaves hospital.'

'I wonder,' Georgia said slowly, 'how Laura and your mother are getting on?'

William rose, collected their plates, rinsed them and put the coffee-percolator on the stove. 'My mother is greatly relieved. Coffee?'

'Yes, please. Will?'

He turned at her tone and their eyes met across the kitchen. 'Yes?'

She tucked her hair back behind her ears, pushed her sleeves up. 'Why did you stay today?'

He held her gaze captive again, and the pause stretched until he said, 'Because I wanted to get you in the appropriate mood to apologise properly, Georgia. And the only way to do it seemed to be to wait until your righteous indignation had subsided somewhat. No—' he held up a hand as she opened her mouth to protest '—you have every right to be indignant, Georgia.'

She hesitated, and thought a little sadly, Do I? *Am I?* 'It was all Laura and Neil's fault really,' she said in a subdued tone. 'And my reputation may be a little to blame, I suppose.'

'Not to mention rather wildly inaccurate.'

She smiled, but unamusedly. 'I didn't realise I was featuring as such a "breaker of hearts—not to mention other things", as you put it.'

'Didn't you, Georgia?' The coffee started to bubble and he poured two cups and brought them over to the table.

She grimaced and regarded her cup. 'Well, I deny being deliberately stuck-up, and I certainly deny—' she raised her eyes to his suddenly '—deliberately leading men on only to dash their hopes, kind of thing—other than Harvey, and I explained about him.'

'But—and you taxed *me* with this yesterday,' he said thoughtfully, 'I'm sure they tend to flock after you.'

'A bit,' Georgia replied, with an airy wave of her hand. 'I usually take no notice of them.' She stopped and grimaced ruefully. 'Maybe that's where the stuck-up bit came in.'

'I see.' William Brady rested his shoulders back and looked amused. 'So this reputation of yours has probably been built on sour grapes or, more precisely, deflated male egos?'

'It would seem so.' Georgia eyed him a little warily. 'I also, when I came to my senses, walked out on David Harper quite dramatically, rather than wait for the reverse to happen. So the appearances of that—of what happened there—could have been misleading.' She shrugged. 'Perhaps that's why people find it mysterious or imagine I'm a real breaker of hearts.'

He smiled, but when she opened her mouth to speak again he said wryly, 'I believe you, Georgia, and I'm proud of you. What I would really like to achieve, though, is some restitution for all the things I've inflicted on you over the last couple of days.'

She frowned. 'What do you mean?'

He regarded her meditatively, then said, 'Turn it into a more positive experience, if I could.'

Her heart started to beat heavily and her lips parted, but at the same time a car made itself heard, driving up to her front steps and stopping, and she closed her mouth and they looked at each other questioningly.

'Expecting anyone, Georgia?'

'No. Oh, unless it's my mother!'

But it was Harvey Wainwright.

'Harvey!' Georgia said exasperatedly as she opened the door to his knock. 'What are you doing here?'

'Come to see you, Georgia,' he replied genially. He was quite tall but rather stockily built, and he wore gold-rimmed spectacles at all times that did not disguise a certain stubborn gleam in his eyes. 'Tried to get hold of you a couple of times on the phone yesterday but there was no answer, so I rang your mother this afternoon and she said you'd tried to go to Sydney but had come back.

She had the feeling there was something mysterious going on, so I thought I'd come and check it out. Did you get my roses, by the way?'

Georgia eyed him irately. 'Yes, thank you. But I've told you, Harvey—'

'I know, I know,' he broke in, and manoeuvred around her so that he was well and truly inside, and it seemed senseless not to shut the front door as there was a cold wind blowing straight in. 'You've told me that you don't want a relationship, but that's fine with me—I can wait. And in the meantime why shouldn't I send you flowers as a measure of my esteem?'

'What I've really told you—' Georgia began pointedly, then stopped as she realised Harvey was suddenly staring fixedly past her. She swung round to see that William Brady had appeared. 'Oh. Um... this is...'

But William strolled up to them, and Georgia was struck silent again for several reasons—but foremost amongst them was the striking difference between the two men.

Harvey was a picture of sartorial elegance, his grey suit well cut and worn with a discreetly pin-striped blue and white shirt and navy blue tie. His black leather shoes shone and his fair hair was as sleek and brushed as if he were just setting out for work instead of having finished a no doubt busy day of litigation.

He would have eaten out, she guessed, and knew for a fact that he was into fine dining, particularly French dishes, which he took great pleasure in pronouncing with a flourishing French accent. He was also into 'obscure but robust' and 'zesty on the middle palate' or 'subtle little' wines. And she knew too that he would be incapable of boiling her an egg.

William, on the other hand, was still in his blue jeans and mulberry sweater, and yet she suddenly knew there was an intrinsic style to William Brady that Harvey would never possess. But it was more than that; there was also the crucial knowledge that he would never bore her rigid as Harvey did...

It was during the seconds when she was grappling with this thought that William said something that caused her to do even more of a mental double-take...

He said, 'Darling, aren't you going to introduce me to your visitor?'

She shut her mouth with a click and turned to Harvey, to see that he had also been taken supremely by surprise. In fact he was rooted to the spot, and more so as William slipped an arm casually about Georgia's shoulders, dropped a light kiss on the top of her head and held out a hand to him, saying, 'William Brady. How do you do?'

Harvey took the proffered hand belatedly, with a dull flush staining his cheeks and his expression slipping from bemusement to a kind of anger. 'Wainwright,' he returned stiffly. 'Harvey Wainwright.' Then he added belligerently, 'I just came to check up on Georgia. Anything could have happened to her in this weather.'

'Oh, she was perfectly safe with me,' William drawled. 'It was quite an adventure, wasn't it, my sweet?' he said, with a lurking smile down at Georgia. 'Would you like a drink?' he added to Harvey.

The implication was obvious, but probably unnecessary—that proprietorial arm around Georgia's shoulders said it all. But when Harvey cast her a bitter, accusing glance as he declined a drink William again chose to make the position plain.

'I'll see you out, then,' he said, with an easy air of possession—the air of a man not only in possession but also in residence. And for once in his life Harvey Wainwright was speechless as he was ushered out.

So was Georgia—struck speechless when the front door closed.

William, however, said, 'That should get the message across,' as he observed her working lips, from which no sound came, and her heightened colour.

'I don't *believe* you!' she managed to say at last.

He raised a wry eyebrow at her and sauntered into the lounge. 'You did want to get rid of him, didn't you?'

'Yes, but not *that* way!' Georgia replied, following him.

'Georgia—' he turned and eyed her critically '—it's neither kind nor honest to continue a friendship with a man who wants you.'

'You know damn well I'm not, William Shakespeare!'

'Then why is he still calling and sending you flowers?' he said simply.

Georgia shut her mouth on an exasperated exclamation. 'All *right*. Perhaps I shouldn't have made the odd use of him, although the other day you seemed to think it was his own look-out if I did,' she said tersely. 'But this way— For one thing it's not *true* and for another it will be all over town! My mother...' she said rather faintly, and added, 'You have no idea what my mother's *like*. She'll hound me to death and probably hound you too.'

'You don't think Harvey will bury his wounded pride in a sea of silence?' he queried.

Georgia said something extremely uncomplimentary, and then, 'Harvey is the biggest gossip you ever met!

He'll find some way to twist it all around. William Brady, you've just become a marked man at your own hands. Congratulations!'

He shrugged and looked perfectly unperturbed. He said, 'Georgia, I think you're overreacting, but will you let me tell you *why* I was prompted to do it, despite my sentiments of the other day?'

She stared up into his hazel eyes and swallowed suddenly as she remembered what he'd been saying before Harvey's interruption. 'Why?'

'Look, sit down. Would you like another cup of coffee?'

She nodded after a moment, and said barely audibly as she moved to the settee, 'Why do I get the feeling I'm not going to like this?'

He paused, looked at her narrowly, then turned away to get the coffee.

'Well?' she said when he sat down opposite her. 'Don't keep me in suspense, Will. I just sense,' she added, 'that it's going to be more of the same. Take courage and go forward, Georgia!' she said, deliberately deepening her voice in mimicry of his. 'Is that what you meant about making this a more positive experience? And why you sent Harvey away with a flea in his ear?'

He looked at her expressionlessly. 'Yes. Is it so impossible?'

She sat back with a sigh and picked up her coffee-cup. 'I suppose not.'

'And instead of encouraging the wrong men— OK!' he said wryly as she started to flare up. 'I accept that he was probably one of those hard-to-squash types, but all the same... Why don't you, instead of leaping back ten paces and projecting an aura of autocracy, not to mention sheer, downright bloody-mindedness, lower your guard a little?'

Georgia drank some coffee, found it very hot, spluttered a little then said with irony, 'You are laying it on the line, Will.'

'You can fall into these things without altogether realising what you're doing. You can allow your bitterness and unhappiness to feed on itself, Georgia.'

'I'm sure you can! Oh, hell,' she said with some despair, 'do you have to preach to me, Will Shakespeare?' And she angrily wiped away a ridiculous tear. 'It's not actually having the desired effect, much as I *appreciate* your desire to improve my lot in life—in fact, I think I prefer it when you're insulting me.'

'Georgia—'

'Well, at least that doesn't make me maudlin!'

'Why maudlin?' he asked, with his lips twisting.

She was silent for a long time, staring at her cup, then she shrugged and said, 'Why? Because you're the only man I've felt like being approached by for a long time. Sorry—I don't know *how* it could have happened, after the way we met and all the rest of it, but it has.' And she lifted her head at last and looked straight into his eyes, her gaze bleak, quite straight and very blue.

He sighed.

Georgia jumped up. 'You don't have to say a word, Will. As a matter of fact you just said it all perfectly without the benefit of words, but, look, it's all right! I didn't ever hold out much hope. But would you mind very much if I called you a taxi now? I'm sure you could put up at a hotel for the night, and I really think that's the sensible thing to do, don't you? Least said, soonest mended, least discomfort all round and that kind of thing, you know?' she said cheerily.

'No, I don't.' He got up and came over to her, but she backed away.

'Oh, no, Will.' Her voice quivered with the effort to keep it bright and breezy. 'No, you don't—not that again. I'll survive, believe me—'

'What do you think I'm going to do?' he said quietly.

She pretended to be flummoxed, then, as if struck by inspiration, she tapped her forehead. 'Kiss me? Kiss me *and* comfort me? Just to let me know I am desirable after all? Is that what you had in mind—or is it still amusing you, Will?'

'No, it's not what I had in mind,' he said evenly, and reached for her.

But Georgia backed away further, only to find that she'd backed herself into a corner, and then her composure suddenly broke. With a sob she tried to thrust past him, but he hauled her into his arms and said roughly, 'Sometimes it's the only way to shut you up. *Don't*, Georgia. I intend to kiss you as I've only ever kissed you—like this.'

'Will?'

'Mmm?'

Georgia moved her head on his shoulder. She was in his arms, on his lap, on the settee. 'Sorry.'

'There's nothing to be sorry for. Feeling better?'

She smiled slightly and he kissed her gently. 'Yes. But I can't help wondering where we go from here—did I make a complete fool of myself?' She tilted her chin so she could look into his eyes.

'Far from it.' He stroked her cheek. 'Did I . . . redeem myself at all?'

'What do you mean?' she whispered.

'Have I made up for allowing you to go on thinking this wasn't something that crossed my mind when we first traded insults, right here in this room? I wondered then whether your skin would feel as smooth as it looks, wondered how you liked to be made love to and what it would be like to have your stunning body under my hands—and I thought that Neil was the last man for you, but could quite understand why he'd fallen for you.'

'Did you honestly? Think *all* those things?'

'Honestly. But not particularly. . . pleasantly, I have to concede.'

'Even when you were telling me I wasn't your type?'

'Even then.'

'So—why?' she whispered. 'I mean, I understand why you might not have liked being attracted to me when you thought I was—all the things you thought I was. But why, tonight, were you trying to palm me off onto other men—so long as they weren't Harvey, of course?' She had tried to sound humorous and wry, but it had come out differently and she bit her lip.

He sighed and laid his head back, then said deliberately, 'Georgia, I'm off to Bosnia in about four days, and I will always be off somewhere. I think it's the way I'm made.'

'If. . .' Georgia paused. 'If the one serious woman in your life had been content with the way you are, would you have stayed with her, Will?'

He narrowed his eyes as if he was looking into the middle distance. 'That's a hypothetical question I can't answer. She *said* she knew how I was, and in the blaze of passion we first experienced she maintained that it didn't matter.

'Perhaps I should qualify that,' he said thoughtfully. 'She knew how important my job was to me, but she didn't realise, she told me later, that she wouldn't even be able to know what I was thinking most of the time. I think that's when it came home to me—how things were with me.'

'Maybe you just weren't right for each other.' Georgia paused. 'Do you think your roving lifestyle has fed this dislike of commitment you have?' She pursed her lips then chuckled suddenly. 'That sounds a bit like the question of what came first, the chicken or the egg, but what I'm trying to get at is whether it's become a habit with you—as it became a habit with me to be the way I was—or whether it stems from your mother abandoning you at an early age to the *untender* mercies, by the sound of it, of a stiff, stern father.'

His lips twisted. 'Probably a mixture of both.'

'You don't seem that concerned about it, Will,' she said after a moment.

'I'm not—other than in *this* context. There doesn't seem to be a lot I can do about it, you see.'

'Well, *I* am—concerned about it,' she retorted.

'Georgia...' He looked down at her with a mixture of amusement and enquiry.

'What's so strange about that? You were concerned enough about me to—well...' She shrugged and didn't go on.

'And look what happened.' He played with a strand of her hair.

Georgia bit her lip, then said huskily and urgently, 'Please don't say you regret it, Will. I can cope with anything but that.'

'Oh, hell,' he said softly, and touched her mouth. 'No, I could never regret kissing you, Georgia. It seems I can't even help myself,' he added rather drily.

'Good,' she said promptly and they laughed quietly together until she asked, 'Are you going to leave it at that, though?'

'Georgia—'

'Will, I'll make you a promise. In four days' time, if you still go to Bosnia—why Bosnia?' She sat up with a sudden frown. 'You're liable to get yourself killed there!'

'It's my job. I have to go, Georgia.'

She settled back in his arms, looking rebellious and afraid for a moment. 'What was I saying?'

'You were going to make me a promise, but—'

'Oh, yes, if you go, when you go—whatever—I promise there'll be no tears or recriminations.'

'Is this your way of inviting me to make love to you, Georgia?'

'Yes,' she said baldly. 'And if you intend to lecture me about it, don't bother. I've always been the kind of person who makes up my mind quickly, and *speaks* my mind. But one thing you can't accuse me of is promiscuity! David Harper was the first, to my regret, but you're only the second, and . . . it's been a long time between drinks,' she finished flippantly, although her eyes were curiously bleak.

'That's not what I'm afraid of—I'm afraid—'

'That my hormones are breaking out?' she said humorously, but also in an attempt to head off what she knew he meant—that he was afraid of her falling in love with him. 'From my point of view,' she added, 'it might be best if they were, Will. Look at it that way. Then you could leave me with my hormones all propitiated and all set to soldier on.'

He was silent for so long she got restive and tried to sit up again, but he drew her back. 'Georgia, don't.'

'Besides which, I think *you* need it,' she said sternly. 'If these continual outbreaks of you not being able to keep your hands off me or whatever other name they go by are any guide. Dear William,' she finished, with a wicked little glint in her eye.

He grimaced.

'Think of your health,' she said then, 'if nothing else. Your mental stability, your general well-being. I could be quite therapeutic for you, in other words, Mr Shakespeare,' she added solemnly, and relaxed as she saw the glint of laughter in his hazel eyes.

'I've got the feeling that ought to be my line, Georgia, and—'

'Why? Do men think they have the sole right to take the initiative?'

'Georgia,' he said firmly, 'this is becoming an impossible conversation.' And he lowered his head and started to kiss her rather urgently.

About half an hour later all she wore was a pair of tiny pearl silk and lace bikini briefs as she stood in a soft pool of lamplight in her bedroom, with the muted shades of ivory, cornflower and lavender all around her.

She was standing in front of William, who was seated on the bed, with her hands on his bare shoulders, although he had not yet removed his jeans. They'd said nothing for a while because words had seemed inadequate as he'd caressed her full, pale, rose-tipped breasts, slid his hands down the slender waist beneath the luscious curves above, almost absently trailed a finger below the elastic of her briefs, causing her to shiver slightly, then cupped her buttocks, which were neat and trim, twin perfect orbs that felt as smooth as satin beneath those hands...

'Will...' she said on a breath.

'Georgia?' he murmured in reply, and raised his gaze from her body to her eyes.

'Will,' she whispered, and, within the circle of his arms, slid her palms down his chest as she sank to her knees between his legs. 'I'm dying slowly.'

'You're not the only one.'

'What will we do about it?' she asked huskily.

'I'll tell you what I'd like to do about it,' he responded barely audibly, and touched her nipples in a way that sent a wave of sheer sensuality through her body to her loins. 'Throw you on the bed and have my very urgent way with you. Sorry,' he said with a wry little smile.

Georgia chuckled. 'Don't be. I was hoping you'd say something like that.'

'On the other hand, we could be more civilised about it.' And he stood up, raising her to her feet as well. 'I won't throw you, precisely.'

'Thanks. Perhaps I can help?'

'I can't imagine anything you could do that hasn't already been done.' He released her, but only to slide his jeans and underpants off.

She caught her breath because William Brady unclothed was rather breathtaking: those wide shoulders tapered to a hard, lean waist and hips and long legs, and the whole was smooth-skinned, apart from some golden hairs on his chest and legs, and discreetly muscled and undeniably powerful—as she already knew...

'I meant,' she said on another breath, 'I really don't mind if we're a bit uncivilised about it.'

'Don't you, Georgia?' He slid his hands beneath her armpits and pulled her against him. 'All the same, I'd rather not be—and we'd be better on a bed...' And he lay down, taking her with him. 'Like this.'

'I see what you mean,' she teased, then grew serious. 'But it's my turn now, Will. Just lie still...'

And she raised herself on her elbow and bent over him as she slid one leg between his and started to pay tribute to his body as he had to hers—with her lips and hands, deeply, quietly and intently, and in a way, had she but known it, that promised unimaginable delight.

Nor did she know that the lamplight made her eyes bluer, her skin more golden and her whole aura in her dedication to pleasing him so different from the Georgia Newnham he knew that it was he who took a sudden breath this time. He grasped her wrists with one hand, held them above her head, turned her onto her back and claimed her powerfully...

'Will?'

'Georgia—are you all right? I'm sorry, I didn't mean to be so—'

She put a finger to his lips. 'Don't say a word. If I hold you like this, could we sleep, do you think?'

His eyes, in the moment before he reached out to turn off the lamp, were amused. 'In a word—yes.'

* * *

They woke a couple of hours later, and some moonlight coming through the skylight laid a sheen of silver over Georgia's hair as she snuggled beneath the covers and moved her body along William Brady's side, laying her cheek on his chest. 'Was I what you expected, Will?'

'No,' he said quietly and stroked her hair.

She grimaced. 'How so?'

'You were like...' he paused '... like Scheherazade—more beautiful than I could believe, then quiet and mysterious. You made me feel like a sultan, you were like a diamond catching the light and reflecting it through me with finally that burst of pure joy but still that hint of mystery.'

'Will...' Georgia said curiously unsteadily, and took a breath. 'Oh, Will. Perhaps you are a Shakespeare after all—I don't know what to say.'

'That could be a first,' he murmured, and drew his fingers down her spine. 'I only hope I pleased you—I probably don't have to tell you what you did to me.'

'Yes, oh, yes, you did please me,' she said in that same slightly shaken voice, and added, 'For what it's worth, I think it might have been something we both needed rather desperately.'

He twined his fingers through her hair. 'You might be right. For someone with a sore back, how is it?'

'Uh—I hadn't thought about it.'

'Like a massage?'

'Love one...'

'It's like silk,' he said a few minutes later. 'Your skin.'

But Georgia had fallen asleep again. He stared down at her hair on the pillow, at the outline of her cheek and the sweep of her lashes on it, and after a long moment closed his eyes briefly, covered them both and lay back himself.

Georgia experienced no regrets whatsoever when she awoke. She snuggled up to him and said contentedly, 'I can hear Brenda but she never comes up unless she's invited. I'm going to have to do a complete about-face, though.'

'In what respect?'

'About you. I wasn't very complimentary.'

'Not to mention accusing me of taking advantage of her.'

'She did tell me she thought you were gorgeous,' Georgia said wryly, 'and that you gave her goosebumps.'

'I can't imagine why.'

'Can't you, Will? I can,' she replied gravely.

He laughed quietly and kissed the top of her head. 'The feeling is mutual.'

She reached out then and did something she'd wanted to do for days—touched that faint white scar on his temple. 'A bullet, Will?'

'No.' He grimaced. 'A cricket ball when I was about fifteen.'

She laughed. 'And here was I thinking it was something terribly dangerous and traumatic!'

'If you'd ever been hit on the temple by a cricket ball, you might agree that it is.'

Georgia hesitated as her mind was suddenly flooded with images of him as a tall teenager, then said a bit abruptly, 'Could we do it again, then, Will?'

'I thought you'd never ask,' he responded.

'You're not quite the kind of lover I expected either, Will,' Georgia said a few minutes later.

'How so?'

'I thought you might be a bit contained about it all.'

'That's a serious charge to lay, Georgia,' he said wryly, but continued to caress her breasts in a way that seriously interfered with her breathing.

'Not really, since you've routed that theory completely. You're a particularly—involved kind of lover,' she said, and added with a tremor in her voice, 'Really intimate and expressive.'

'It's really hard not to be when confronted with all this perfection.' He trailed a hand down her flank and then up the curve of her bottom. 'You're a work of art.'

'How are my bruises?' she asked ruefully.

He inspected them, running his fingers over them gently. 'Fading. Still sore, though?'

'Hardly at all.'

'Have you any preferences for how we conduct this lovemaking, Georgia?'

'No, Will,' she replied very quietly. 'I'm completely in your hands.'

It was raining again, and the early morning light was pale and murky, so he switched on her bedside lamp and the beautiful colours of the room, the ivory, lavender and cornflower, sprang into soft radiance. As did the disarray of her bed, the swathe of her hair on the pillow and the different tints of their skin against each other as well as the planes, angles and curves of their bodies.

'You're also a bit of a work of art, Mr Shakespeare,' Georgia said huskily, sliding her hands down his back

towards his hips. 'Like a sculpture. It's going to be hard
not to visualise you without your clothes now.'

'I've had that trouble since I first laid eyes on you.'

'So you told me last night.' Her mouth curved. 'You
hid it so well, though, Will.' And she moved away a bit
and stretched her arms above her head and pointed her
toes.

He propped his head on his hand, glanced down her
body then into her eyes, and said, 'Do that again,
Georgia.'

'I . . .' She gestured. 'I was only doing it to stop myself
from leaping on you,' she confessed. 'I feel like—yodel-
ling, or something like that.'

'Are you a yodeller?' His lips twisted.

'No. Never. I avoid it like the plague at all times—
that's what you do to me, Will Brady.'

'Will you stretch for me again, Georgia? It does all
kinds of things to me.'

So she did, and he traced a devastating path down her
body between her breasts with their erect, flowering
peaks, over the soft mound of her belly to the triangle
of curls at the base of it, and she lowered her arms suddenly and buried her face in the curve of his shoulder,
saying barely audibly, 'It's too much, Will.'

'I'm afraid it is for me too, Georgia,' he answered
equally quietly, and moulded her hips to his. 'Sorry. . .'

'Don't be sorry,' she gasped. 'I'm loving it.'

They slept again afterwards, for about an hour, then she
felt him leaving the bed and reached for his hand. 'Will?'
She brushed her hair back. 'Where are you going?'

'To make us breakfast.'

'Are you starving again?'

He smiled wryly down at her. 'It is ten o'clock.'

'Oh, no!' Georgia sat up with a frown and pulled the sheet over her breasts. 'Oh, dear!'

'What?'

'Well, I was going to see Brenda and—do all sorts of things!'

'All sorts of things?' he said quizzically, looking down at her hand still in his.

'Maybe not all sorts of things,' she conceded with a grin. 'But Brenda—'

'I told Brenda last night that you were really tired and would probably sleep in.'

'Did you, now?' She started to frown, but it became another grin and she lay back, still holding his hand. 'That was pretty good thinking, Will!'

'Not that I had this in mind at the time, but—'

'I know—you don't have to explain. Never mind, what do they say about the best laid plans?'

He looked into her eyes with a wicked little glint in his own. 'That was Robbie Burns, not Will Shakespeare.'

'I know that!' Georgia said grandly, but lifted his hand to her mouth and kissed his knuckles, then let it go. 'OK, you can make me breakfast, Will—if you'll let me cook you dinner tonight.'

'With pleasure.'

'Off you go, then,' she commanded. 'I have certain plans of my own.'

'Such as?'

'I'm going to... lie here and imagine that I really am Scheherazade,' she said, her eyes sparkling, but then she sobered abruptly and bit her lip. 'I don't mean—'

'Georgia—' he slipped his hand under her hair around her neck and leant down to kiss her gently '—you really are in some ways. I meant that, but—'

'I know, I know.' She turned her lips to the palm of his hand as he slid it forward again. 'Don't take any notice of me, Will.'

They stared at each other and he started to say something, but the phone rang and the moment passed.

It was Laura; Georgia heard him say that she wasn't handy at the moment, and she pulled a pillow into her arms and hugged it to her.

CHAPTER SIX

'GEORGIA? Is that you, darling?'

'Mum, of course it's me. Who else would it be?' Georgia said into the phone with a grimace. She'd had breakfast in bed, bathed and it was now nearly lunchtime.

'You sound a bit different, that's all,' her mother said blithely. 'Georgia! You won't believe this, but Laura has left James—apparently he was all but mistreating her and Adrian is furious, absolutely furious. By the way, darling, Harvey is worried about you.'

There was a short, tense little pause, then Georgia said dangerously, 'Mum, don't tell me Harvey has been on to you *again*!'

'Yes, he has—rather early this morning. He told me all about William Brady.'

'He doesn't *know* all about William Brady!'

'Well...' Her mother paused delicately. 'He did meet him last night, didn't he? Georgia, I would love to meet William Brady! Why don't you bring him round for dinner this evening? Your father would love to meet him too.'

'No, I can't do that, Mum. He's off to Bosnia in a couple of days, anyway.'

'Georgia—'

'Mum, look,' Georgia said rather gently, 'I'm fine; don't worry about me. Bye for now. I'll be in touch.' And she put the phone down with a sigh.

William was right behind her and he took her in his arms as she turned, and touched her mouth lightly. 'So you were right.'

'Yes. Don't be surprised if she comes calling. My mother is—' she shrugged '—*lovely*, but a bit of a trial at times.'

'We could go away,' William suggested.

'Where? It would need to be a long way away,' she said humorously. 'Besides which we'd still have to drive, probably. No, Will, I think we'll stay put. You'll just have to be brave if she turns up.'

'I'm quite happy to be brave. It was you I was thinking about.'

Georgia grimaced. 'She may take the hint—my father is often a restraining influence on her—and to be perfectly honest I have neither the energy nor the inclination to be anywhere with you but here. Don't forget it's only a day or so ago that you drove me all around the backblocks of New South Wales and Southern Queensland!'

'I haven't forgotten,' he said wryly. 'As a matter of fact, I can think of nothing nicer than being here with you at the moment, so—'

'Good. We'll just have to work out a way to repel all invaders— Oh, no! I don't believe this,' she said incredulously as she glanced out of the window at the sound of a car pulling up—a very large car.

'Your mother? That was fast work. Georgia—'

'Not my mother. The only person who could be worse than my mother—my uncle Adrian,' she said faintly.

'Judge Adrian Newnham,' William murmured with a rueful twist of his lips. 'Might he have come about Laura?'

He had.

'Georgia,' Adrian Newnham, who was immensely tall, bald and not above frightening the life out of anyone whose misfortune it was to be in his courtroom, be they defence or prosecution, let alone criminals, said sternly, after knocking thunderously on her front door, 'I want to know exactly what's going on! Where the devil is Laura now?'

'Hello, Uncle Adrian—uh, didn't she tell you? By the way, this is—'

'I'm not interested in who this is!' Adrian Newnham barked. 'My only daughter is missing, I'm about to have James Moreton, the scoundrel, clapped in irons, and you try to introduce complete strangers to me! I don't know what the world is coming to, I really do not!'

'Uncle Adrian,' Georgia said soothingly, 'Laura is quite safe, believe me, and I wouldn't advise you to clap James in anything at the moment. It's nothing to do with him that—uh—Laura's not here. It's—entirely her own affair, as a matter of fact.'

'Georgia, I've known you since the day you were born, so don't try to fob me off—you were the last person to talk to her, from what I can gather, after which she disappeared off the face of the earth—how can it be entirely her own affair? Am I not her *father*? Am *I* not the one supposed to be rescuing her from a miserable marriage? How could she do this to me?'

'Strangely enough, Laura *can* do the odd—odd thing from time to time,' Georgia replied with some irony, and sighed. 'It's really not my place to tell you this, Uncle Adrian. I mean to say—'

'*Georgia!*' Adrian Newnham bellowed.

'If you'll excuse me, sir,' William Brady said a little drily, 'but your daughter has fallen in love with my half-brother, who recently had a serious accident, and she is at his bedside in Sydney at the moment.'

Adrian Newnham swelled, turned a dangerous shade of purple and said, 'And who might you be, young man?'

'William Brady,' Georgia put in hastily. 'William *Spencer* Brady, Uncle Adrian—'

'I don't care what kind of a Brady— What did you say?'

'Judge Spencer Brady's son,' Georgia said. 'An acquaintance of yours, I believe, Uncle Adrian. I know he was at Mum and Dad's wedding.'

There was utter silence for a moment or two as Adrian Newnham subjected William to the most intense scrutiny—something he bore with placid equanimity—then, to the surprise of them both, Georgia's uncle said with much less ire, 'Hmm! You don't look much like him, nor your mother, who ran off with an artist if I recall—silly girl. Had a bit of a soft spot for her myself, y'know—or maybe you don't.

'Half-brother,' he mused, then swelled again. 'Do you mean to tell me Laura's fallen for that utter reprobate's *son*? The painter chappie? Some foreign name? This goes from bad to worse—how could she do this to me? At least James was a solicitor!'

'But a bit of a cad in other respects by the sound of it,' Georgia reminded him, trying valiantly not to laugh.

'Don't remind me,' Adrian said through his teeth. 'And now this. Who would ever have daughters?' he added bitterly, then did an astonishing about-face.

'Why couldn't it have been you, young man? I like the cut of your jib, although I don't know you from a bar of soap. I had a great deal of respect for your father and, well, I've told you about your mother. Why couldn't she have fallen for you? But of course!' He struck his forehead and advanced upon his niece. 'Georgie, my dear girl, I'm very happy for you. At least one of you has managed to get it right at last!'

But before he reached her, and as her mouth fell open, his mobile phone beeped in his pocket. He withdrew it, conducted a brief, trenchant conversation with his secretary, and said, 'I'm due in court; I have to go. But will you tell Laura to get in touch with me before this day is out? And I *mean* that! In the meantime, I'll ring your mother, Georgia, and reassure her. She was in a bit of a twitter over you when I rang her to try and track Laura down. Goodbye!' And he left.

They watched the large car drive off, then Georgia buried her face in William's mulberry sweater and laughed until she cried. 'I do apologise,' she said eventually. 'He's quite sweet beneath all that—they all are, our family—but—'

'"Who would ever have daughters?"' William quoted, with a smile lurking at the back of his eyes.

'I know,' she agreed ruefully. 'First me and David, now Laura and James and *Neil*—'

'And now you and me,' he completed, and sobered.

'Yes.' Georgia sighed. 'I wouldn't blame you if you took fright—and flight.'

He released her, stared narrowly down into her eyes, then took her hand. 'Not today—unless you want me to?'

She took an unsteady breath—of relief. 'No.'

'Then what would you like to do today?'

She thought for a bit and then drawled with an American twang, 'Could I show you around my spread, mister?'

'With pleasure, lady,' he replied.

So they spent the next few hours doing just that. In fact she saddled Wendell for herself and Connie for William and they sallied forth.

'Well, Will,' she said, looking across at him approvingly, 'you have a good seat.'

'Thanks,' he replied wryly, 'but I haven't ridden for years.'

Later he said, 'I'm impressed, Georgia—there's only one thing this place lacks.'

'What's that?'

'Some kids and some dogs,' he said with a teasing grin.

She grimaced. 'Dogs are a bit of a problem; Connie hates them. And as for kids, as I said to you once, I'm only twenty-three.'

'Do you like kids?' he asked after a moment. 'Would you like to have a large family?'

'Yes, I would rather. I get on well with kids—especially once they're walking, talking and *riding*. I give a class at the local pony club once a week—I think I told you that—and I help out with disabled children at a special riding school.

'Despite the fact that I'm an only child, I come from a long line of large families, and I seem to have inherited the tendency to want to— I don't know.' She shrugged, then glanced at him with a glint of a smile. 'Perhaps it's the managerial streak that you once accused me of having, Will.

'Damn,' she said as some raindrops fell, 'it's going to rain again. We'd better get back!'

They only just made it, and as they put the horses away she told him about the additions she had planned for the stables: two more stalls, accommodation and a bathroom for a permanent groom, an enlarged feed and tack-room and an office.

'The plans are drawn up and I've got council approval—if only it would stop raining!' she said ruefully as the afternoon grew wetter, darker and colder.

'I know what we'll do,' she said once they were upstairs. 'Since it's well past lunchtime, I'll make us tea and scones.'

'Tell me more about your plans,' he said some half an hour later, when they were drinking tea and eating hot scones dripping with butter and honey.

Georgia required no further prompting. 'Well, I want to expand in two directions. I want to take on more horses to spell—I have the space for another five paddock yards—but what I'm really keen to do is start breaking in young horses. As yearlings, when they get to the sales, they're broken-in enough to lead and be handled, but then someone needs to teach them to be ridden.'

'Something that requires a lot of patience, I imagine.'

She looked at him with a lurking grin. 'Contrary to what you may be implying, I have endless patience with horses, Will.'

'I believe you. I wasn't implying that at all.'

'Good.' She was still smiling. 'Anyway, that's why I'm planning these extensions. I'd definitely need some full-time, live-in help. Now—' she finished her tea and moved to sit cross-legged at his feet '—tell me some more about *you*.'

'There's not a lot to tell.'

'There must be. Where do you live? You must have some sort of a home base.'

'I have a large house on Sydney Harbour that I inherited from my father. I avoid rattling around in it as much as possible.'

'Why don't you sell it? Why don't you find somewhere you could be comfortable and happy? You could even find yourself wanting to stay put more often.'

He regarded her with a wry little look. 'You're no doubt right, Georgia.'

'Well, why?' she persisted seriously.

'I don't know.' He shrugged. 'I'll get around to it one day.'

Georgia watched him in silence for a moment, then a glint of amusement lit her eyes. 'Can you imagine Uncle Adrian and your mother being sweet on each other? Not that I know your mother, and it might have been wholly unreciprocated, but it's just hard to imagine him being sweet on anyone! Laura's mother died when Laura was in her early teens and there's been no one since that I know about. What about your mother? What happened after Neil's father deserted her and your father wouldn't have her back?'

'I think she decided she'd got her fingers burnt often enough. She's been alone ever since.'

'What's she like?' Georgia asked, her head tilted curiously.

'She's...' he paused '...still very attractive—she was seriously beautiful as a young woman—still the very affectionate, demonstrative person she always was, and still haunted by the guilt of being unable to live with my father, who was the complete opposite, and having to leave me.'

'He must have been a very hard man,' Georgia said with a little shiver. 'And so well respected,' she marvelled. 'Did he ever have anyone else?'

'No.'

'Was he still in love with her, do you think?'

'Yes.'

'Will,' Georgia whispered, 'that's so sad!'

He grimaced. 'They were better apart, Georgia. They were such complete opposites and, much as I respected him and loved her, even I hated the kind of hell they created for each other. I take it your parents don't have those problems?'

Georgia sat back and grinned. 'My mother and father are inseparable, much as my father claims my mother drives him mad. She's one of those really naïve people who refuses to believe the worst of anyone—she fusses a lot and she's crazy about her garden. She not only talks to her plants, she also writes them notes.'

He raised a quizzical eyebrow. 'Notes?'

'Uh-huh. It used to be a bit of a trial to me when I brought friends home to find the rose bushes with these little notes stuck on their thorns—"Darling, you're looking beautiful today" or "Take heart, petal, I vow I'll get rid of these aphids!"'

'Seriously?'

'Seriously,' Georgia said, but lovingly. 'You probably think she's mad, but she's only a bit eccentric.'

'I was thinking that I'd like to meet her.'

'Who's to know that you won't?' Georgia looked heavenwards humorously. 'But my father would give her

the moon if he could.' She sobered. 'They really care
about each other.'

William smiled and reached out a hand to touch her
hair. 'And they have a lovely daughter.'

'Thanks.' She sighed. 'I've been a bit of a trial to them,
though. Who would have daughters?'

'Come here,' William said quietly.

She rose after a moment and sat down on the settee
beside him. 'More words of wisdom, Will?' she said,
with another lurking little smile.

'No. Much simpler—I couldn't keep my hands off you
a moment longer.'

She laughed and lay back in his arms. 'I can't take
issue with that!'

They made love then and Georgia lay on her front
afterwards, with her head resting on her arms, and said
huskily, 'Will? Why do I feel as if I've been dropped
from a great height?'

His hand wandered down her body and came to rest
on the curve of her bottom. It was still raining outside
and the light coming through the skylight laid a bluish
tinge over her lax limbs. He moved his hand upwards
again, this time to gather the tangle of her hair and push
it aside so that he could see one eye, and he smiled down
at her.

His sunlight-after-rain smile seemed to go right to her
heart, so that she turned over and sat up suddenly,
pulling the sheet around her.

'What?' he said quietly.

'Nothing...' She lay back in his arms and tried to
compose herself. 'Well, just that poor Brenda will be
feeding up on her own again.'

But as Georgia soaked in the bath later she found her composure and energy renewing themselves, as she mentioned to William Brady, who happened to be in the bath with her.

'I knew it was a good idea to have a king-sized bath,' she added with a grin.

He looked around at the wall of mirrors, at the cornflower tiles and thick lavender towels. 'Your bedroom and your bathroom are stunning. A fitting setting for you.'

'A fitting setting for what you once thought I might be, Will,' she reminded him. 'I quite clearly remember you raising your eyebrows very expressively when you first saw them, as if they reminded you of a—a seraglio.'

'I've never seen a seraglio,' he said, and soaped one of her legs.

Georgia laid her head back and swished the bubbly water idly. 'Provided I was the only inmate, I wouldn't at all mind being Scheherazade to your sultan, Will. Specially when you do that,' she added dreamily as he turned his attention to her body.

'It's probably meant to be the other way around in seraglios,' he teased.

Georgia sat up. 'If you're inviting me to return the compliment, I have to tell you I'm suddenly full of energy, Will!'

He groaned and laughed. 'I don't know if I'm up to that.'

She splashed him until he caught her and forced her arms to her sides, claiming her mouth in a long, lovely kiss. 'Only teasing,' he murmured when they drew apart at last, with the most wicked little glint in his eyes as he drew his hands down her slippery body.

'I knew that,' she said pertly. 'But I'll tell you something else—I'm really going to be Scheherazade now.'

'Oh? How?'

'I'm going to get out of this bath and leave you alone in it and I'm going to concoct you a delightful dinner. And that may wear me out again to the extent that, I might not be up to anything of this nature until...' she tipped a hand from side to side '...who knows?' she finished airily.

'Things of *this* nature?' he suggested ingenuously, moving his hands.

'Will,' she breathed erratically, 'that's not fair. I might be good for *nothing* afterwards—not even dinner.'

'Very well, I shall desist—don't forget I didn't have lunch.'

Her mouth dimpled at the corners, although she said severely, 'If that's not cupboard love, I don't know what is. You're as bad as Connie. Well, I'm going.' And she kissed him briefly and leapt out of the bath.

And that was how she came to prepare dinner while William watched television peacefully. She also went down to check on her horses, and found them peaceful too. When her rack of lamb was nearly ready and smelling delicious she was suddenly possessed of an idea. The table was set, this time with crystal, silver and linen, the vegetables were on, the dessert was made, and she judged she had about twenty minutes...

She went into her bedroom and said over her shoulder before she closed the door, 'Won't be long, Will. Why don't you pour us a drink?'

He looked up and raised an eyebrow, but she shut the door gently and strode across the bedroom to open her wardrobe.

Fifteen minutes later she stared at herself in the mirror and was happy with what she saw—a fine ivory long-sleeved wool dress that came to her ankles and clung to her figure, worn with a broad bronze leather belt to emphasise the slenderness of her waist. She also wore bronze shoes with little heels and her hair was swept up into a severe pleat.

There were drop pearls in her ears, pearls around her neck and a chunky gold and pearl bracelet on her wrist. Her face was made up carefully, her perfume was by Dior and, despite achieving it all in record time, she didn't look rushed.

She took a deep breath and walked towards the bedroom door to make a grand entrance—just as the phone rang. She stopped and heard William answer it, expecting him to call her. But he didn't. She opened the door quietly and saw him with his back to her, talking rather intently into the instrument and making notes on the back of an envelope.

'Get me there via Sydney,' she heard him say. 'I need a couple of hours there, then after Dili on to Jakarta, where I can pick up a flight to Rome or Athens. Yes... No, it's too late tonight, I couldn't make it into Brisbane in time, but first thing in the morning. Yes... No... You can ring me back here. Bye.' And he made a few more notes on the envelope before turning with a frown in his eyes.

'Will...?' Georgia said out of a suddenly dry throat.

His eyes narrowed as he took in the lovely dress, the elegance of her hair and how it emphasised the patrician bone structure of her face, the careful make-up, the radiance of the pearls that complemented the fine, clear texture of her skin, and she thought he sighed as he said,

'A looming emergency in East Timor, I'm afraid. I have to fly to Dili tomorrow and—'

Georgia moved. 'And then on to Rome or Athens for Bosnia. Yes, I heard. Well! It's just as well I prepared a feast, isn't it?'

'Georgia...'

But she smiled at him wryly and said, 'Don't say a thing, Will. Let's just savour the moment.' And she turned to walk into the kitchen.

She managed to keep up a bright flow of small talk as they ate the lamb, which was delicious, and a lemon meringue pie she'd whipped up, but when they were finished her conversation dried up as William cleared the table, put the coffee on and sat down opposite her.

'Georgia.' He put his hand over hers as it lay, looking lonely and lost to her, on the table.

She swallowed and looked away. Then she said barely audibly, 'It's over, isn't it, Will? Oh, well, perhaps it's for the best.'

'There's no reason why we shouldn't keep in touch,' he said quietly.

'Yes, there is.' It came out fiercely and she bit her lip. 'I mean, I would rather you didn't, Will. I think a clean break is best. I...' She paused and grimaced. 'I'm not sure what you had in mind—making me your Australian lover, perhaps—but I couldn't do it. If I learnt nothing else from David Harper, I did discover that's not the kind of thing I'm built for, and that's how you yourself seem to read me. Now.'

'Yes. Georgia...' his eyes were sombre '...I wish I could tell you how much I regret this.'

She managed to smile at him although her eyes were full of tears. 'That I fell in love with you? No more than

I, Will . . . No, I can't regret it entirely, so you don't have to worry. I'll be fine.'

But when he got up and came round to draw her to her feet and take her in his arms she wept into his shoulder for a minute or two, then drew away. 'There,' she said shakily, but with some of her old spirit. 'The storm's over. Sorry. You know, I'd like to think I . . . did something for you. Eased some tension, gave you a bit to laugh about—some positive things, at least.'

'And I'd like to think you knew just how much you did do for me, my dear.'

'Just not the one thing I would have liked,' she whispered, but took hold of herself again immediately. 'Will—' her voice was husky but the tears were stemmed '—what I'm going to suggest now might seem a bit strange, but—if there is a flight you can catch tonight, I'll drive you to the airport.'

He still had his arm around her shoulders and she felt him tense. 'Georgia, I—'

But she said with quiet desperation, '*Please*, Will.'

He tilted her chin and looked into her eyes, then closed his briefly. 'All right. But you don't have to drive me. I can get a taxi—'

'No. It'll take hours to get out here, for one thing.'

'Georgia, it's raining and—'

'That doesn't worry me. I can call in to see my parents on the way home—even spend the night with them. It's about time I got back to them; they'll be dying of curiosity,' she said ruefully.

He touched her mouth lightly, with a frown in his eyes. 'What will you tell them?'

She shrugged. 'That Spencer Brady's son is one of the nicest men I know—but not for me.'

'Georgia—'

'No, Will, that's all there is to it,' she said stubbornly, and stood on her toes to kiss him—just briefly. 'Now, will you use the phone while I pack a bag or do I have to do it for you?'

'I'll just drop you here,' she said.

Brisbane Airport was aglow with lights that were alternating between being magnified and distorted through the raindrops on her windscreen then clear and sparkling as the wipers clicked backwards and forwards. Georgia was still wearing her ivory dress, with a raincoat thrown over it.

William Brady didn't get out of her four-wheel drive immediately.

'Will,' she said with difficulty, 'you haven't got much time.'

'Georgia...' his hand closed hard over her wrist warningly '...just let me say this. If I could change myself for anyone, it would be for you. If there is any—blame for all this, it lies with me.' Then he released her wrist and picked up her hand, saw the turmoil in her eyes and said, 'I won't make it any harder if you'd rather I didn't.'

'I would...rather you didn't, Will.'

'Goodbye, then, my Scheherazade.' And he kissed her palm and opened the door.

The last Georgia saw of William Brady was the back of his tall figure, with the tweed jacket swinging from his wide shoulders as he strode through the terminal doors.

*   *   *

A week later Laura came to see her with the news that she was moving to Sydney. She had only come back to collect her things; Neil would be released from hospital in a few days and she would be moving in with him to look after him.

'How is he? Any lasting effects from the accident?' Georgia asked as she made them coffee.

'No. Thank goodness.' Laura accepted her cup. 'Although it'll be a while before he's back to full strength again. Georgie, I didn't get a chance to apologise properly, or to thank you for working it out.'

'Well, I should imagine it would have got worked out once Neil was lucid—even if William had managed to get me to his bedside.'

Laura curled her legs under her on the tartan settee. 'I can't believe it all happened like that—can you?'

'I certainly found it most bewildering at the time,' Georgia said with some irony.

'Sorry again.' Laura looked rueful. 'When you're desperately unhappy, scared and confused, you obviously don't think too straight.'

'No.' Georgia sipped her coffee. 'Not to mention when you're madly in love. How has James taken your defection?'

'Not very well. Not that I've seen him, but he told Dad I was a cold, stuck-up bitch and he'd be glad to wash his hands of me.'

Georgia blinked. 'Well, that took some courage!'

Laura half smiled. 'Did you know Dad insisted on coming down to "vet" Neil, as he put it?'

'Yes, Mum told me. I hesitate to ask what it was like.'

'Funnily enough, it went very well. Neil's mother was there— Georgie, you're not going to believe this, but—'

'I know.' Georgia grinned. 'He once had a soft spot for her. He told us the morning he came here to find you.'

'Well, I've got a very funny feeling that my future mother-in-law could become my future stepmother—they got on like a house on fire! He took her to dinner, he took her to lunch—he even took her to breakfast!'

Georgia's grin faded.

But Laura appeared not to notice as she continued, 'Which brings me to William Brady—Dad seemed to have the crazy idea that you and he were engaged or something!'

Georgia swallowed a lump in her throat. 'I know,' she said casually. 'He was in one of those impossible moods—he even asked William why *you* couldn't have fallen for him. He liked the cut of his jib, he said.' She grimaced. 'And he left before we could explain things to him.'

Laura was silent for a moment before she said slowly, 'He *is* nice. He came to see Neil before he flew to East Timor, or somewhere like that. Did you know he's a famous author?'

'What?'

Georgia stared at her cousin, who happened to glance at a book still lying on Georgia's coffee-table entitled *Micro, Mela and Poly*. She picked it up and said, 'I see you do! Did he give it to you?'

Georgia's lips parted. 'Do you mean to tell me William Brady is B. S. Williams?'

'Yes! It's his name backwards—Brady Spencer William with an S added. His mother is so tremendously proud of him—she was the one who told me. And Neil is too, now, although—'

'Yes, William told me,' Georgia said mechanically.

'And weren't you the least bit interested, Georgie? In William Brady?' Laura asked rather intently.

'Oh, no,' Georgia heard herself say brightly. 'You could say we took an instant dislike to each other.'

'That's not what Harvey Wainwright has been putting around town.'

Georgia managed to laugh. 'Well, if William did one thing for me, he got rid of Harvey. No, Laura. Our Will Brady is a loner—although, you're right, a nice one.'

'I see,' Laura said thoughtfully.

'How on earth have you had time to catch up with Harvey's gossip?'

'My beloved aunt Sonia—your mother, in other words,' Laura said succinctly.

Georgia groaned. 'I told her—'

'She didn't seem to believe you.'

'So she sent you on this fishing trip?'

'Darling, by now you must know all the ways and means of this family! She's worried about you. And, seeing as I got you into this, I wondered if I could help. She said you spent the night with them, the night William flew to Sydney, and she said she hadn't known you all your life not to know when you were deeply disturbed about something—despite your explanations about William Brady which made the whole thing sound quite hilarious.'

Georgia stood up abruptly. 'Laura, can I just say one thing and will you leave it then? It's over. It was never meant to be in the first place. He's not for me.'

'But you would have liked him to be?'

'Yes ... *Laura*—'

But Laura was on her feet, putting her arms round her cousin. 'Georgie, I'm so sorry. I feel as guilty as hell. But don't bottle it up; I won't tell a soul, I swear.'

Georgia stopped shaking after a minute and said wearily, 'There's not a lot to tell. He warned me right from the beginning and I made him a promise that I intend to keep. Look, I'll get over it—I've these extensions planned and more horses coming—did I tell you I'm going into breaking in yearlings? So I'll have plenty to occupy me.

'As a matter of fact I *was* getting over it, but the thought of you marrying his half-brother and Uncle Adrian marrying his *mother* whilst I ... I guess it just got to me. But you're right.' She managed a smile. 'It could only happen in this family!'

And suddenly they were hugging each other and laughing together.

Laura spent the rest of the day with her, and when she left she looked at her searchingly as she said, 'Feeling a bit better?'

'Much better. Thanks, pal.'

'If you need someone to talk to, just give me a call.'

'I will, I promise.' And she waved Laura off then went upstairs.

The book on the coffee-table seemed to leap up at her, and she picked it up, then cradled it to her breast and wandered into her bedroom, seeing in her mind's eye the times they'd made love. And she knew that she would never be able to tell anyone how bereft she felt, how hurt, at the fact that William Brady hadn't even told her he'd written the book she held in her arms.

Over the next couple of months, her extensions started to become a reality. She fenced off five more paddock yards and was able to fill them with no trouble, and she took in her first two yearlings to be broken in. She worked like a Trojan and gave herself no time to sit around and mope. Indeed, she gave herself little time to think about anything but horses, about her spelling farm and its growing reputation. She even put off hiring extra help.

It all came crashing down with a fall from an excitable young horse which left her with a badly broken leg and the prospect of never riding again.

CHAPTER SEVEN

'MUM, I want to go home,' Georgia said wearily. 'You can come and see me every day, if you like, but I'm missing my horses dreadfully. I rang Brenda's parents and they're quite happy for her to stay with me for a couple of weeks; it's school holidays anyway. Please, Mum!'

Georgia's parents looked at each other and her mother began, 'Darling, you've still got the cast on—'

But her father broke in, 'If it's what you really want, Georgie.'

'I do, Dad,' she said tremulously, and added with an attempt at humour, 'And I'm handling this old cast and these crutches as if I was born to them now!'

So her parents took her home and spent the morning with her, and her horses welcomed her back so enthusiastically that she stood before Constancy's stall with tears in her eyes.

Then she shook her head resolutely and hobbled over to inspect the downstairs additions to the stables, which had become a reality after the accident at her parents' insistence—although mostly in a bid, she suspected, to give her something to think about while she was convalescing.

Now, built on to the stables, she had an impressive office, an extended feed and tack-room, two more stalls and accommodation for a groom. This was not quite the simple room and bathroom that had originally been planned, because her mother had taken a hand in the decorating of it and the office in another bid to occupy her daughter.

She'd spent hours bringing Georgia sample swatches of material for curtains, blinds and bedspread, carpet samples, books of wallpaper, furniture catalogues and so on. She'd also remarked more than once that Georgia had an eve for decorating, and when on one occasion her daughter had looked at her out of defeated, pain-filled eyes she'd said, 'Georgie, darling, I know you're wondering if this is all a waste of time, but have faith, pet.'

Do I have faith? she wondered, the day she got home, as she looked out of the office window towards the empty paddocks. Empty now because it had been impossible to carry on the spelling farm without her. Do I believe I can build it all up again, ride again, let alone walk properly again? Do I want to? All I seem to want is to be alone...

But Brenda was installed in the spare room upstairs in case Georgia got into difficulties, and because she knew her mother would worry herself sick otherwise.

When Brenda went to bed early that night, Georgia sat for a long time in the darkened lounge, thinking again about her prospects—something she hadn't been able to do in the two months since the accident.

Or at least she was trying to, but she realised that what coming home had done was to open the floodgates of her mind on another subject, and she laid her head back and felt the tears that still came ridiculously easily trickle down her cheeks because—and this was something she had not expected—his presence was so strongly etched into these rooms that it might have been only yesterday

that she had loved and lost William Brady instead of
months ago.

What roused her from this sad reverie was the sound
of a car below, stopping, then driving away, and she
frowned, reached for her crutches and got to the front
door, which was open to catch the breeze on this hot
summer night.

At the same time the man she'd had on her mind lifted
a hand to tap lightly on its panels. William Brady, in
other words, casually dressed in khaki trousers with a
pale green knit sports shirt highlighting those wide
shoulders. William Brady, with his brown hair lifting in
the breeze, his hazel eyes resting on her intently, his
beautiful hands, lean torso and the whole streamlined
height of him standing on her doorstep.

'You!' she gasped, rocking on her crutches and all but
falling until he caught her. 'What are *you* doing here?'
she added angrily. 'Come to view the wreckage? Well,
you can just go away again.'

'Georgia,' he said evenly, his hand still on her arm,
'I didn't know about this until yesterday, believe me.'

'Well, now you do know, and there's nothing you can
do for me, Will, so we'll just have to call that taxi back—
as you see, I'm not capable of driving you anywhere at
the moment.'

'I'm not going anywhere tonight,' he said drily, and
stepped past her to switch on the light, which enabled
her to see two bags on the doorstep—one of clothes, the
other a briefcase. 'Or tomorrow or the next day. In fact
I might as well warn you, Georgia, I've come to stay,
and there's nothing you can do about it. Why don't you
sit down? You look as if you need to.'

She turned fully towards him, her expression stunned, and he looked her up and down narrowly, and started to say, 'My dear, I'm sorry—'

But Georgia knew how she looked—thin and pale, with deep shadows under her eyes and none of her former gloss—and she broke in, 'I don't want your pity, Will, and I certainly don't want you here.'

He merely shrugged, picked up his bags and moved them to the lounge floor. 'I believe the spare bedroom up here is occupied tonight, so I'll sleep downstairs. Can I make us a cup of coffee—?'

But she broke in again. '*How* do you know the spare room is occupied? Or that there's anywhere to sleep downstairs?'

'I spoke to your father.' He went into the kitchen and put the kettle on.

'Do you mean to tell me he—*agreed* to this?' she said incredulously.

William Brady looked across at her a little wryly. 'He—both your parents, as it happens—agreed that I should be allowed to put my case to you. You see, Georgia, I find myself in the embarrassing position of not being able to live without you.'

'No,' she said disbelievingly.

'It's true.' He got out two mugs.

'Well, I don't believe you. I *know* what it is: pity. But I'll be fine, Will, just you wait and see.'

'That's my Georgia,' he murmured. 'All the same, I'm staying. I've got a book to finish, I need a bit of peace and quiet to do it, and this will suit me fine.'

That did it—the mention of his alter ego that he'd not seen fit to confide to her... 'Then I'll go,' she said with quiet determination. 'That should sort things out.'

He put the kettle down and walked over to her. And her heart turned over in her breast—because he looked exactly the same and because she doubted she'd ever get over William Brady—but to have to accept his pity was more than she could bear.

'Georgia,' he said, and her lips parted as she read a determination greater than her own in his eyes, 'you're going nowhere. Because this will not only give us the opportunity to work out whether you can live without *me*, it will also give me the opportunity to *help* you.'

'How?' she said bitterly.

'Have you thought of giving riding lessons to get you over the next few months until you can get into the saddle and take up the reins of the farm again?'

Her eyes widened. 'No...' She licked her lips. 'But...' She couldn't go on.

'Well, I discussed it with your parents and it seemed to all of us to be a good idea. You're in the perfect position here for it—you couldn't find a horsier area or as many people with their own horses. You have a schooling ring, you have all the equipment, and with someone like me on hand to help, as well as Brenda, I don't see why it shouldn't be a success.'

Georgia opened and closed her mouth, then swung her crutches and took herself to the settee, which she sank down on dazedly. She shook her head a couple of times and at last said, 'No. No, Will, it wouldn't work.'

He placed a mug of coffee in front of her. 'Why not?'

She shot him a look of savage impatience. 'Because I don't *want* it to work. Your timing doesn't make things believable, for one thing. For another, I simply can't visualise you running a riding school. What about Bosnia or Chechnya? What about all the famine-plagued nations out there for you to be reporting on?'

'I've seen enough famine-plagued, war-torn, earthquake- and flood-ravaged countries to last me a lifetime,' he replied wryly, and sat down opposite her. 'I've also sold my Sydney home and don't take possession of my next one for a week or so—so I'm footloose and fancy free.'

'You sold your home,' she said slowly, 'but you didn't hear about me until yesterday?'

'I was overseas until the day before yesterday, Georgia,' he said evenly. 'The negotiations were conducted on my behalf by my solicitor. I've been uncontactable for the last eight weeks, which is why neither Neil, Laura nor my mother was able to let me know about you—something I'm sure they would have done in the normal course of events.'

'Where were you?' she asked involuntarily.

'The Falklands, South Georgia and Tristan da Cunha.'

'I've never heard of the last one,' she said drily.

'It's in the South Atlantic, roughly halfway between South Africa and South America. It's very wild and beautiful, with millions of seabirds. There are three main islands in the group: Tristan, the only inhabited one, Nightingale and Inaccessible.'

'Sounds like a good place for you, Will.'

'It might have been once,' he agreed. 'They call the town Edinburgh, on Tristan, and they had to rebuild it after an earthquake in 1961. South Africa has a weather station there, although the islands are administered by the UK and are part of the St Helena group.'

'Of Napoleon fame?'

'The same, but a long way away. I have some wonderful photos.'

Georgia stared at him, then laid her head back. 'Is that how you're going to handle this, Will?' she said wearily.

'How?'

'Like a brick wall—like a charming, impenetrable brick wall?'

'Probably.' He smiled slightly.

'Well, I'm going to bed, but I can assure you that tomorrow I will have worked out some way to get rid of you.'

'OK. Do you need any help?'

'No, Will, it's the last thing I need from you.'

To her surprise she fell asleep quickly and slept deeply and dreamlessly, despite the inconvenience of her full cast on a hot night on top of everything else. And she was awake when there was a tap on her door and William brought her a cup of tea.

She said nothing, but perhaps the look in her eyes told him how she felt. Not that it inhibited him to any extent.

'Georgia,' he said, sitting on the side of the bed, 'the sooner you stop feeling sorry for yourself—no—' His hand shot out and arrested her wrist as she reached for her tea to fling it over him. 'You'll drink that, my dear. One cup of coffee has used up my entire store of patience towards you emptying things over me. And the sooner you get up, the sooner you can get to work. You have two pupils arriving this morning.'

Her mouth fell open. 'You're joking!'

'No, I'm not.'

'Who? How?'

'The—er—Davidson children, I believe. They're bringing their own ponies.'

'Do you mean those two little monsters who live down the road? But this is unbelievable. How did you arrange that so soon?'

'It was your mother's suggestion. *Their* mother is the daughter of a friend of your mother's. Apparently they've been dying to have some lessons from you. It's also school holidays and they're driving their mother mad. She was delighted to consent to lessons every morning this week for them.'

'But...'

'I'll be with you all the way, Georgia. Breakfast will be ready in about twenty minutes.'

I don't believe this, she thought an hour later. But the fact of the matter was that she was dressed, in a denim skirt and white blouse, she had a shady hat on, and she was sitting on two bales of straw—just the right height to be comfortable. She was also issuing instructions to Leila and Daniel Davidson as they cantered round her schooling ring on almost identical ponies.

William was lounging beside her and Brenda, who'd woken to find the object of *her* dreams back in residence, and was consequently in a flush of happiness, was standing by as well.

The lesson lasted an hour, with the twins behaving impeccably, although once off their ponies they reverted to their normal practice of verbal abuse of each other, not to mention pushing, shoving, pinching and hair-pulling.

'For heaven's sake get rid of them, Will,' Georgia said, although with a grin.

'I'll ride home with them,' Brenda offered.

'Well?'

'Well, what, Will?' Georgia said wearily, when they were upstairs and he was making lunch, having given her a cool drink.

'Was that so bad?'

'No.'

He glanced across at her critically. 'I've asked your parents to dinner tonight. Feel up to it? You can rest this afternoon.'

She said nothing.

'I didn't mean, this morning, that you were being anything less than incredibly brave, Georgia.'

'Thank you,' she murmured, but the words were loaded with satire. 'What did you mean when you accused me of feeling sorry for myself, then?'

'I meant in relation to us.'

Georgia gasped. 'Look here! You were the one who walked out of my life—'

'You were the one who promised me I could,' he said quietly.

'Don't remind me, but I *kept* that promise. So why shouldn't I object when you come walking back into it—?' She stopped abruptly.

It was his turn to say nothing.

It was she who said, 'So you reckon I'm feeling sorry for myself, feeling hard done by and ill-used and determined to extract every last bit of agony out of it? You're not quite right, Will. The thing is, I *know* you, and I know what this is, and I know there's no question of us spending the rest of our lives together. But, if you care to stay on until you can be convinced of that, be my guest.'

She closed her eyes, not altogether believing that she'd said what she had, but a moment later was possessed of a cold determination to prove to William Brady that she could either live with him or without him; it didn't make much difference.

'Laura is—of another opinion,' he said after a long pause.

The one thing Georgia had prayed for since William Brady had stepped back into her life was that her cousin Laura had not got hold of him. When she opened her eyes and found his hazel gaze resting on her she knew that it had been a vain prayer.

'That was four months ago, Will,' she said casually, and decided to go for broke. 'If I remember rightly, at the time I was conscious of the irony of things. Of Laura and Neil, and my uncle Adrian and your mother. I've got over that.'

'Have you got over making love to me and wanting to yodel?'

'I haven't had any desire to make love to anyone for a while,' she said, but couldn't hide the flash of anger that lit her cornflower eyes. 'Listen, just do me a favour—stay or go, but spare my parents this evening. I don't think they'd enjoy it.'

'You don't think you owe it to them to lessen the load a bit?'

'What do you mean?' she asked through her teeth.

'Your mother showed me her rose garden yesterday. There were little notes on the bushes. They were all addressed to you, with expressions of love and concern.'

'Oh...' She stared at him until his image blurred as tears flooded her eyes, then she buried her head in her hands.

She didn't have the strength to resist when he sat down beside her and took her in his arms, although she said, 'Please don't...'

'Georgia,' he said, making no attempt to kiss her but holding her thin body as it was racked with sobs, 'let me help.'

And how is it going to help me when you go away again? she asked, but only of herself. And that, of course, was the awful truth she was trying to hide from him.

'I don't seem to have much choice in the matter,' she said huskily, a long time later.

'No.'

'You're a hard man, Will Shakespeare. Just promise me one thing—*no* more of this.' She managed to say it firmly and she thought he sighed.

He did kiss her then, but only the top of her head, then he answered the determination in her eyes with a smile in his own. And he didn't answer directly, only said ruefully, 'My lunch could be ruined.'

'Cold meat and salad? I doubt it.'

So they got into the habit of riding lessons in the morning and William working on his book in the afternoon while Georgia rested or pottered around or vice versa—he wouldn't let her teach all day.

Brenda stayed on with them at Georgia's invitation and as the days passed and word got round, almost like wildfire, she found that the appointment book that William had bought for her began to fill up—not only with children still on holiday but also with more experienced riders eager for her advice, on their riding and on their horses.

William built her a higher chair on a platform that she could get up to fairly easily, and he installed a sunshade over it.

'Didn't know you were so good with your hands, Will,' she said flippantly.

'No? Comfortable?'

'Yes, it's comfortable, and it gives me a much better view. Thanks.'

'You're welcome.'

Georgia glanced down at him and swallowed suddenly because the strong, tanned lines of his exposed throat did curious things to her. She covered her reaction immediately by climbing down carefully with his aid and saying, 'I'll be able to dance on these crutches by the time I get the cast off.'

'Just promise me you won't get up or down there without me to help you,' he demanded.

'I promise.'

And because she was grateful she said to him, for the first time, that evening after dinner, which he had cooked and Brenda had cleared, 'How's your book going?'

'Well, thanks.' They were watching television, she on the settee, he sprawled out in an armchair, while Brenda, who had loved every minute of her stay and was wishing it didn't have to end the following day, hummed as she ironed in the kitchen.

'Are you using a typewriter or what?' Georgia asked.

'A lap-top computer. Care to come down and see my set-up?'

Georgia hesitated, then reached for her crutches.

'This,' she said wryly a few minutes later, looking around the groom's bedroom, 'became much grander than it was supposed to be.'

'I thought it had a bit of your flair stamped on it.'

'It was my mother's way of keeping me occupied,' she said, but was thinking that the orange-red and pale jade colour scheme, which was repeated in the bathroom, *had* been a good idea. 'Not a bad idea to have a desk in here either as things turned out,' she added, thinking her thoughts aloud as she studied the compact computer on the rather lovely pale oak desk her mother had picked up at an auction sale.

On one side of the computer there were neatly stacked manila folders of notes and on the other an open folder of large photos.

'Will,' she said on a sudden breath, looking closer, 'they're stunning!' And indeed they were: panoramas of cliffs, sea and birds, grassy lowlands and craggy uplands. 'I didn't know you were good at this too.'

He grimaced. 'Photography has always been one of my hobbies, and it's handy to be able to do your own work.'

Georgia thought back to the photography in his book *Micro, Mela and Poly*, which had also been stunning, and said a little drily, 'I once suggested you could turn to cooking if you gave up journalism. I had no idea you had so many strings to your bow, of course.'

'Laura told me,' he said quietly.

'What did she tell you?' she asked warily.

'How upset you were when you found out I was B. S. Williams. I'm sorry.'

She looked at him expressionlessly. 'Laura seems to have bared my heart to you. She and Neil are still happy, aren't they? They've been up to see me a couple of times.'

'Yes, they are. To be honest, I don't know why I didn't tell you, Georgia.'

Georgia looked at him standing before her in his jeans and yellow T-shirt with his arms crossed. 'I know, Will. You didn't want to get too involved with me.'

He started to say something, then stopped and drew forward a basket chair. 'Sit down for a while, Georgia.'

She shrugged and did so. He sat on the bed and surprised her by saying, 'It's gone well these last two weeks, hasn't it?'

'Very well,' she agreed. 'You've charmed my staff— well, you'd already achieved that—and you've charmed my pupils. I'm sure most of the girls over twelve are violently in love with you, and when you go I could find that their numbers diminish alarmingly.'

She stopped and thought for a bit, about her mother and father and how, that first evening when they'd come to dinner, it had been clear from the expression in their eyes that they hadn't known whether they'd done the right thing, and how their painful concern had prompted her to let them know that she and William had made no decisions but that she was happy to have his help. She'd also guessed—correctly, although she'd not verified it— that many anxious family conferences had taken place on the subject of her and William Brady.

She couldn't deny that she was looking a little better, was obviously happier and more relaxed with something dear to her heart to fill her days, and that the change had not been lost on her parents, who still visited nearly every day.

She looked up from her thoughts with a grimace. 'You've even charmed my parents, and on top of all that you've made me some money.'

But he refused to take offence, only said with a half-smile, 'Think what I could do for you in a lifetime, Georgia.'

'You're not persisting with that line, are you, Will?' she said quietly.

'Yes, I am.'

'Then tell me this. What happens when your book is finished?'

'I thought we could go to where I've planned to set my next book—Cape York Peninsula, the Gulf and the huge cattle stations in the area. As a matter of fact I have an interest in one.'

'Something else you didn't see fit to tell me.'

'No. I accept the charge,' he said quietly. 'But by the time I've finished this book you should be out of that—' he glanced at her cast '—so we could have a holiday. Or a honeymoon.'

'Funny you should say that. I quite thought you were going to at least try to explain why it was so difficult to tell me you were B. S. Williams.' Her gaze was very direct and bright with anger.

'Unfortunately, you got it in one go, Georgia. I didn't want to get too involved with you. But that was then.'

'Well, the only thing that's changed is this, Will.' She tapped her cast.

'No, it's not. One of the things that changed *me* was an island called South *Georgia*. I'd found it difficult enough to put you out of my mind, but once there it was impossible.'

'Isn't it a barren, bleak sort of place?'

'Yes. And with an Antarctic climate that sees three quarters of it covered with perpetual snow. It also has penguins, seals and introduced reindeer, as well as millions of birds. But all the time I was there I thought of you and all your fire and grace. And I began to know that although I'd finish the trip and go on to Tristan da Cunha—I'd already contracted to do this book—I couldn't walk away from you, Georgia, as I'd thought I could.'

'That's easy to say now, Will.'

'It's also true.'

'Well, thank you for saying it. But—I mean it could have been South *Carolina* and you might not have had the problem!'

For the first time she detected a glint of anger in his hazel eyes, and was shaken by a wave of pleasure—although almost immediately she was nearly as horrified as she'd been pleased.

But he only stood up and said easily, 'OK. Like to go back to television?'

'Why not? There's not a lot else I can do, Will.'

'Oh, yes, there is,' he drawled. 'You could put aside your ill-used feeling and once Brenda goes to bed we could play some music, talk, then lie in each other's arms and sleep. It would probably do you the world of good, Georgia.' He smiled at her coolly. 'In the meantime, I'll do some work. But I'll help you up the stairs first.'

'I can manage the stairs, Will—don't touch me,' she said through her teeth, and left with all the fury she could muster on a pair of crutches.

It was no wonder she came to grief. And it was fortunate that he was right behind her, so that he caught her as she missed her footing and started to tumble down the stairs. All the same, she knocked her head on the railing and got her wrist caught in a crutch, twisting it painfully.

And she had to suffer him saying, 'You bloody idiot, Georgia Newnham,' before she blacked out.

CHAPTER EIGHT

WHEN her eyes fluttered open both Brenda and William were looking down at her with expressions of acute concern. She was laid out on her bed and the first thing she said, groggily, was, 'Sorry, that was my fault.'

William sat down beside her, his anger apparently forgotten, and took her hand. 'How do you feel?'

She winced and he narrowed his eyes and looked down at her wrist. 'You may have sprained this, and you got a bump on your head, but how does your leg feel?'

'The same,' she said cautiously. 'I don't think I did any damage to it.'

'All the same, the doctor's coming.'

'I'm sure I don't need—'

'Yes, you do,' he said gently. 'Better to be safe than sorry.'

And that was how he was all through the next day, though he acceded to her request that they didn't bother her parents when she'd had an X-ray to make sure she hadn't done any further damage to her leg. Which she hadn't. Indeed, she got the news that the breaks were almost healed and she would be able to have the cast off in a matter of weeks. And then he made her dinner that evening—their first evening alone.

Her wrist wasn't badly sprained but it had a support bandage on it. Other than that, all she had was a slight headache. They had mentioned nothing of the events that had led up to her fall all day, but as she nursed a glass of wine, and while he did the dishes after dinner, she said musingly, 'Will, how are we going to go on?'

'How would you like to go on, Georgia?' he said after a long pause.

'I would *like* to feel I wasn't feeling ill-used and sorry for myself but I can't, and I would like to believe you but I can't do that either. So—I don't know.'

'Then how about just letting me hang around?' he suggested.

That brought a strange little smile to her lips. 'Do you really believe you can wear me down?'

'No. I'm not going to take anything for granted about you ever again.'

'That's nice,' she murmured.

He came over then and topped up her wine. 'I've also decided that I won't mention a thing about us not being able to live without each other until you're fighting fit and back to your old, inimitable self. How does that affect you?' He sat down opposite her and she thought she saw the old, wicked little glint in his eyes for a moment.

'That sounds like reverse psychology.'

'One uses whatever means one can,' he replied.

But a spark of interest that she couldn't hide lit her eyes, and she said with something like her old vigour and decisiveness, 'You're on, Will! I never could resist a contest—which is what I suspect this is.'

'I didn't say a word about contests,' he drawled.

'Ah, but I'd be surprised if I was wrong!'

He shrugged. 'So I can stay?'

She cast him a pithy look. 'Don't come all innocent with me, Will. Short of throwing you out, I have no choice.'

'Sorry.'

'No, you're not. Anyway, tell me something about your life as a writer—how you got into it, et cetera. We might as well indulge in some civilised conversation.'

'I always wanted to write. My father always wanted me to be a lawyer. So we compromised. I did law and an arts course and when I still had no ambition to be a lawyer he didn't so much agree as realise he had no choice, so he gave in gracefully to journalism.'

Georgia raised an eyebrow. 'You wasted a lot of time on something you didn't want to do.'

'Not really. I learnt a lot and it's a good background for exploring the frailties of human nature,' he said with a wry little smile. 'And one isn't greatly equipped to be writing in one's early twenties, which was something I learnt the hard way.'

'How come?'

'Well, I thought I had the definitive literary novel in me then. I now know I'm much better at this kind of thing.' He gestured to his book, which still reposed on her coffee-table.

'Do you make a lot of money from it? That's your third or fourth, isn't it?'

'Third. Enough.'

'Still,' she mused, 'not trooping around the world reporting wars and seeing the truth of things for yourself is going to take a bit of replacing in your life, I would have thought.'

'There's a time and tide in one's life. I'm not saying all journalists are, but it's an occupation which can render you permanently cynical.'

'Not to mention unwilling to be tied down.'

'Even *unable* to be—after too many years of it. Not to mention whisky-soaked and a few other things. It is also a bit worrying to find that the habits of your work, which in this case consist basically of observing others, can make you into a permanent fringe-dweller.'

They looked at each other, Georgia steadily, he with a disconcerting lack of any humour in his eyes.

'Of course you'd always travel, though,' she said at last. 'To research the kind of books you like to write.'

He shrugged. 'Yes. But in my own time and at my own pace. And since I resigned I've been offered a syndicated weekly column on local current affairs and a weekly feature in a British paper. Have you got anything against travel? Some travel? Especially if you had someone living in here to look after things for you.'

She grimaced and looked at her cast. 'There's some doubt that I will ever be strong enough to run a spelling farm again.'

'But there's always the hope that you will.'

'Yes. Yes,' she said at last, and looked at him with a grin. 'Sorry to say this, Will, but I'm going to bed. I'm not only tired but I have this headache—self-inflicted, but all the same...'

'I think it's a good idea. By the way, I'm so well set up downstairs I might as well stay there. And now you've got a phone extension down there you only have to give me a call if there's any problem.'

'Good thinking, Will!' She reached for her crutches but he stood up and helped her to her feet and handed them to her.

He didn't leave it at that. He took her chin in his hand when she was balanced and said, 'Goodnight, Georgia. Sleep well.' And he kissed her on the mouth, a slow, gentle kiss as he stroked her cheek, which mesmerised her strangely and evoked all sorts of memories.

'Will...' she protested when he lifted his head at last and his fingers left her face. 'You promised...'

He smiled slightly. 'I promised I would *say* nothing on the subject. I made no other promises.'

'That's...' She stared up into his eyes and was nearly overwhelmed by everything about him—his shoulders and lean hips beneath a blue and white striped T-shirt and jeans, the remembered feel of his skin beneath her fingers, his body on hers... Her eyes darkened. 'That's so like a man,' she said contemptuously.

A little glint of amusement lit his hazel eyes. 'If it's any consolation, this man is going to find it extremely hard to get to sleep tonight, Georgia. Goodnight, my dear.' And he turned away.

Georgia shut herself into her bedroom as she heard him finish tidying up the kitchen and, finally, the front door open and close. It was only then that she swung on her crutches over to the mirror on her wardrobe door, where she studied herself critically.

There was still a faint flush in her cheeks, but there was pain and bewilderment in her eyes. Then she looked down at her cast and for the first time gave thanks for it, because without it who knew what might happen?

It wasn't strange that she found it difficult to get to sleep as she examined the new dilemma she faced. Her examination took the form of realising that when she'd first got home she'd mourned the loss of William Brady in a mostly spiritual way, mourned not having been able to break into his innermost sanctum. Even when she'd been presented with him again that had still been her greatest sense of loss, and she'd tried to cloak it behind a façade of outrage.

But now it was different. Perhaps it had been growing, but now it was going to be a distinctly physical torment too, she knew, and put her fingers to her mouth because the feel of his lips was still there. She could breathe the heady, masculine essence of him as if he were at her side—and feel her body stirring for him. Her poor, battered body that was still too thin, still clothed in plaster from the top of her thigh to her toes on one side—her body which had not interested her in the slightest for more than four months.

And she drew a pillow into her arms and thought, What the hell am I going to do now?

It didn't help that there was moonlight coming in through the skylight so that some of the lovely colours of the room were just discernible, and it was not hard to think in the silvery light of Scheherazade...

She had herself better in hand the next morning. Or thought so until, after a hot, dusty morning's tuition, she was dying for a shower, which she couldn't have, and to wash her hair.

She was cursing her cast beneath her breath and running her hand distractedly through her hair while William made them tea and lunch.

'What?' he said over his shoulder.

'I haven't been able to have a shower or a bath for nearly *three* months,' she said bitterly. 'Even to have a sponge-down I have to put my leg in a garbage bag and tie it at the top. Washing my hair on my own is a nightmare—and I'm itching like mad beneath this stupid thing. That's what!'

'I see,' he said gravely. 'Could I help you wash your hair at least?'

'No.'

'Georgia—'

'I can manage,' she contradicted herself moodily.

'Have you done it on your own yet?'

'Not really. My mother or Brenda has always been on hand.'

'Well, tell me how they've done it.' He paused. 'Actually, I think I know. Didn't Brenda rig up a chair for you in the bathroom?'

'Yes,' Georgia said ungraciously.

'Why don't we try that? After you've had your sponge-down and when you're appropriately clothed again, in case you're afraid it all might be too much for me,' he suggested innocently.

Georgia regarded him fiercely, then swore briefly and warned him, 'Just don't try anything, Will. I'm liable to bite.'

'I'll remember that. Give me a call when you're ready.' And he turned back to the lunch he was preparing.

So Georgia got through the awkward business of sponging herself down without wetting her cast, dressed in a green cotton skirt and matching blouse, tucked the collar in and called for him.

He came armed with a chair that was low enough for her to lean back in against the basin, with her leg propped out in front of her.

'Uh-uh,' he said when she was finally positioned in the most comfortable way she could be, 'there's a slight problem of logistics here. The taps don't reach your head. How do hairdressers get around that?'

'They have a hose attached to the taps, Will,' she said tartly. 'What you need is a jug.'

'Of course, how dumb of me,' he marvelled, and went to get a jug. 'All right, next step, Miss Newnham?'

'I can't believe you're that dumb, Will! You wet my hair, trying not to drown me in the process, with *warm* water, so that you don't either scald or freeze me,' she said irritably.

'Coming up—there, how's that?'

'It's—OK,' she admitted grudgingly. 'Now you get the shampoo—don't use too much—and rub it into my hair.'

'Like this?' he said after a while.

Georgia opened her eyes as his long fingers massaged her scalp with a firm, relaxing pressure, and caught him looking down at her with amusement. She sighed. 'Lovely, Will, I have to say, but before we get carried away, would you mind rinsing it off and putting some conditioner on? It's right there next to the shampoo.'

So he repeated the process and again massaged her scalp in a way that was impossible to resist. 'I suppose you're really laughing at me now,' she said, with her eyes closed again.

'I wouldn't dream of it.'

'Yes, you are!' And her mouth trembled at the corners. 'I probably deserve to be laughed at a little, because the truth is I feel like a new person. You'd better rinse this lot off now, Will, before I . . . fall asleep or something.'

'Yes, ma'am.' And when that was done he helped her to sit up and dried the excess moisture out of her hair with one of her lavender towels, picked up her comb and combed it all neatly, then struck a pose. 'Who knows— another string to my bow?' he suggested with a quizzical grin.

For the life of her she couldn't help it—she found herself laughing back up at him. 'No, a hairdresser is the last thing I can see you as, Will. Stick to emulating Shakespeare. Thanks for that, though,' she added, but with her smile already fading.

It hurt her heart, already hurt from memories of them together in this bathroom, to see this side of Will Brady again—a side that would be lovely to live with... 'Well, let's have that lunch,' she said gruffly, and pushed herself out of the chair.

It was by coincidence that she saw another side of him a few days later.

She was tutoring a nineteen-year-old boy with plenty of potential but rather a high opinion of himself and a streak of temper he tended to take out on his tall, strong horse. She reprimanded him twice, then tried to explain how his impatience was communicating itself to the horse, making it fidgety and uneasy, not to mention a lethal weapon.

For a while things progressed normally, until the horse stumbled again. The rider swung viciously on its mouth and lashed it cruelly with his crop, causing the inevitable—the horse reared and kicked explosively, doing its best to dislodge the rider—and Georgia was powerless to do anything.

Moreover, with her heart in her mouth, she had to watch William stride up to it, quite sure he would get caught by the flailing hooves.

He didn't. He put an iron hand that reminded her of the semi-trailer collision on its bridle, and with a soothing voice managed to exert enough mastery over the thoroughly overwrought animal to calm it until it stood shivering but obedient beside him. And then in the

coldest, most cutting voice he ordered the boy off and
tore such strips off him that the previously swaggering
nineteen-year-old was all but reduced to tears.

And Georgia, on her high chair, which she was forbidden to leave without his help, stared with parted lips
at this strong, cold man who'd exhibited such fearlessness. The fearlessness didn't surprise her; what as-
tonished her was his brutally contained anger, which
rendered him almost unrecognisable from the laid-back
William Brady she'd thought she knew.

He loaded the horse into its box, refunded the cost of
the lesson and ordered the boy off the property, never
to return. He still had a white shade about his mouth
as he came to help Georgia down.

'Will,' she said tentatively, once she was on terra firma,
'that was very well done. I thought you might get yourself
killed.'

He glanced at her unamusedly, then quite un-
emotionally told her she looked pale and tired and should
go upstairs where he would join her when he'd helped
Brenda feed up. She hesitated, but did as she was bid.

She was positively deluged with phone calls for the
next few hours—her mother, enquiries about riding
lessons and so on. By the time she glared at the phone
and dared it to ring again the sun had set, Brenda had
gone home and William was starting dinner.

Georgia looked at his tall back as he worked at the
sink, then went to sit at the kitchen table. 'Are you all
right?' she said at last.

He turned briefly. 'Fine. Shouldn't I be?'

'Well, you're a bit quiet, that's all.'

'You were talking on the phone for so long, I gave
up.' He went back to peeling potatoes.

Georgia propped her chin on her hands and said after a bit of thought, 'You're in a thoroughly bad mood, Will Brady. That surprises me.'

'It shouldn't. You saw what happened.'

'Oh, I don't mean that. I thought you were wonderful, not only with the horse but also with that young man. If that doesn't teach him, nothing will. I just— didn't expect you to be still mad.'

'I'm not.'

'Now, Will,' she said ruefully, 'who are you kidding?'

'All right,' he said abruptly as he rinsed the potatoes and started to slice them, 'if you must know I don't usually lose my temper like that.'

'I'm sure it was in a good cause, so I wouldn't worry.'

'Yes, well, coming from someone who's normally as uninhibited and flamboyant as yourself, you probably wouldn't.'

Georgia raised her eyebrows. 'How did *I* get in on the act?'

He leant back against the sink, folded his arms and eyed her grimly. 'You were already there.'

She narrowed her eyes. 'What do you mean?'

'You can't be that naïve, Georgia,' he said drily.

'I think I must be, because I have no idea what you're talking about. Unless . . . you've discovered the old wanderlust is not so easy to subdue as you thought? And you're dying to get away?'

'It has nothing to do with that—what the hell do you think I am?' he said roughly.

'You tell me, Will.'

'OK, I'm seriously bloody frustrated, and tired of these games we're playing.'

Her lips parted and her eyes widened. 'I don't believe you . . .'

'Try me, then,' he said shortly.

'I couldn't . . .' She licked her lips. 'Not that it's an option, even if I could—'

'I'm not suggesting we sleep together until—'

'Thank you,' she said with irony.

He eyed her with a look of contempt and strangely that caused her to feel a curl of amusement instead of outrage. I don't know why I'm enjoying this, she thought, but I am . . . 'Are you saying,' she murmured, propping her chin on her hands again, 'that if it hadn't been for me you wouldn't have been prompted to take the actions you did this afternoon, Will?'

'Of course I would have,' he replied scathingly. 'Not quite so excessively, however.'

'I see.' She regarded him gravely until he swore and turned back to the sink. 'I don't know what to say,' she said then.

'Nothing would be preferable,' he retorted. 'Why don't you go away and do something else?'

'Like what, Will?' she said gently. 'No, I think I'd rather have this out. You don't honestly expect me to believe you find me desirable now?'

She saw the way his hands stilled, and he lifted his head to look out of the kitchen window. Then he turned slowly and stared at her intently.

'I'm as thin as a rake,' Georgia continued quietly, and added from the well of honesty within her, 'We both know I was never pretty, and I could limp for the rest of my life—whereas you are the stuff girls' dreams are made of. Have you considered that you might just need a woman—any reasonable woman, Will? But preferably *without* the inconvenience of a plaster cast. They may not have been too thick on the ground in the Falklands, South Georgia or Tristan da Cunha.'

'Georgia...' He came across to her, removed her chin from her hands, insisted she rise and steadied her with a hand on her waist. 'You were always pretty lethal with your tongue, but let me prove one thing to you, if nothing else.'

And he took her in his arms, saying when she moved convulsively, 'Don't waste your time. And don't say another word.'

It was a long, intimate kiss that he subjected her to, made all the more difficult for her because he knew exactly how she liked it—knew, for example, that when he kissed her throat first it made her shiver with pleasure. Knew that when he held her against his body with her head on his shoulder and slipped his fingers through her hair or stroked the line of her cheek and neck it did the same. Knew *exactly* where to slide his fingers down her body, following the curves and communicating to her even through her clothes that he knew all her satiny, secret, sensitive hollows...

So it wasn't much of a contest. When he finally allowed them to draw apart, her breathing was ragged and her eyes confused, even apprehensive, because she'd been kissed thoroughly and she'd been unable to withhold a response or maintain that it was against her will.

'So you see, sweet Georgia Brown,' he drawled, his eyes keen and acute as he noted the look in hers, the colour in her cheeks, the way her breasts rose and fell, 'you may insult me all you like, but if I were you I'd re-examine some of your premises. You might just find you've got the wrong end of the stick.'

Georgia was silent, although she longed to say something along the lines of, What did that prove? Or repeat, That's so like a man! Yet something held her back, something in his hazel eyes that puzzled her, something ironic, but—she couldn't quite put her finger on it.

'Would you like a drink?' he said blandly then. 'Dinner won't be long.'

'But... but you've barely started,' she pointed out unevenly.

'Oh, it won't take me long to put together some steak, egg and chips.'

'All right,' she said slowly. 'Thanks.'

After dinner he suggested a game of Scrabble.

Georgia eyed him thoughtfully. 'Are you sure? Wouldn't you like to get to your book? Or one of your columns?'

'No. I worked all morning. Thank you all the same,' he replied courteously.

But it's there again, Georgia mused as he got out her Scrabble board and set it all up. That something I can't put my finger on...

'Georgia?'

'Ah,' she said, coming out of her reverie. 'I have to warn you I'm a very innovative Scrabble-player.'

'I wonder why I knew that?' he said with a grin. 'In which case we'll have to come to an agreement.'

'Such as?'

'Are you prepared to abide by this dictionary?' He held up her battered old school dictionary which he'd found in the bookcase.

'Well—I guess so.' She grimaced.

'Then let us begin. Are you comfortable?'

'Thank you, yes,' she said formally, but there was a gleam in her eye which told William Brady, did she but know it, that she was thoroughly on her mettle.

They settled down to play and their scores were level for the first half-hour, then Georgia scored a triple with an X and drew ahead. She couldn't disguise how much this pleased her. Once he got up to make them some coffee and put some music on, but for the most part they both concentrated deeply and there was little conversation. Then, to her annoyance, he steadily started to peg her back, and finally he beat her by ten points.

'I suppose,' she said, throwing her wooden letter-holder down disgustedly, 'I could console myself with the thought that words are your business.'

'You could,' he agreed gravely. 'But I thought you were a worthy opponent.'

She laid her head back with a grimace, then raised it almost immediately and said, her eyes sparkling, 'Cards could be a different thing, however.'

He looked at her with a smile twisting his lips. 'Tomorrow night, then?'

'You're on, Will,' she replied promptly, and added, 'Funnily enough, I don't feel tired.'

'It's only nine-thirty.'

'I know.' She laid her head back again. 'All the same, it's the first night I haven't felt like burying myself away early—for a long time.'

'That's a good sign, Georgia.' He collected up the Scrabble and put it away. He didn't sit down as he said with an odd gleam in his eye, 'What would you like to do now?'

She raised her arms above her head, 'Oh, talk...' But she trailed off a little awkwardly and sat up.

'Why not?' he said quietly. And he came round the coffee-table to sit down beside her on the settee.

She felt herself tense, even more so as he picked up her hand and threaded his fingers through hers. But all he said, mildly, was, 'Fire away, Georgia.'

She compressed her lips, then had to smile ruefully. 'That's done it. I can't think of a thing to say.' And she found herself blushing like a schoolgirl as she stared down at his lean brown hand.

'I've had another idea.' His words were barely audible. 'I kissed you earlier with a certain amount of chagrin. I'd like to do it again in a...should we say...better spirit?'

'Will, why are you doing this to me?' she whispered, then, as his mouth hardened, went on in a rush, embarrassed but stubborn all the same, 'Look, I may have been—I may have carried on like a spoilt child at times, but I'll always be grateful for what you've done for me these past few weeks. Couldn't we—shouldn't we leave it there, though?'

'No.' He said it quietly but quite definitely. A faint smile touched his mouth. 'Nor is there anything for you to get all uptight about, Georgia. Look on it as a salute between two friends, if you like.' And he withdrew his hand from hers, but only to slip it around her shoulders and draw her down so that her head was resting on his shoulder.

Georgia breathed agitatedly, then deliberately took hold of herself. 'If this is a way of making me sorry for what I said earlier—'

'Which bit?' he asked amusedly.

She looked annoyed and replied tartly, 'You know which bit!'

'The bit about the Falklands, South Georgia and Tristan da Cunha—and the fact that I may have had to remain celibate while I was there?'

'Precisely!'

'Unfortunately—' he laid his head back and fiddled with her hair '—and much as I'd like to tell you differently, you hit the nail on the head. There were two reasons for it, though. Women weren't too thick on the ground, as you surmised, but even had they been there in their hordes they wouldn't have been any good to me. That was the real problem.'

'Why?' she said wearily. 'Don't tell me it was because they weren't me, Will. I'm the girl you slept with right here and had not the slightest difficulty walking away from.'

'That's not true, Georgia—'

'Oh, yes, it is, Will!'

'And you're never going to let me forget it, are you?' he said, with the suggestion of a drawl in his voice.

'I really don't see why it should upset you in the slightest. I made you a promise and I kept it; I played the game your way. Look, do I have to keep repeating myself?'

He tilted her chin so that he could look into her eyes—and it was there again. That look she couldn't decipher, although this time it was accompanied by some lazy amusement. And instead of saying anything he bent his head and kissed her very lightly on the lips, but didn't press the matter.

Frustration caused her to make a kittenish little sound, but he simply went on fiddling with her hair, and changed the subject. 'Your family is being very circumspect.'

'Thank heavens,' she said devoutly. 'Not Mum and Dad, I don't mean them, but I can't imagine how Uncle Adrian, for example, is managing to contain himself.'

'He obviously feels you're in good hands.'

'He would! And I can't understand why Laura hasn't rushed up here—to give things a shove along!'

William laughed. 'As a matter of fact I asked her to stay away.'

Georgia looked up at him ominously.

'Did you want her up here giving things a shove along?' he enquired innocently.

Her expression defied description for a moment, then she laughed. 'No,' she said, and subsided against him.

They stayed like that for a while, then started to talk desultorily—about the boy William had ticked off so comprehensively that afternoon, and about the thin, earnest twelve-year-old girl called Jane, who had turned up out of the blue one day with an offer to clean out stalls after school in exchange for some riding lessons. She had no horse of her own and they'd discovered she'd walked three miles from home, so they'd put her up on Wendell on a leading rein and Georgia had had to hide the tears in her eyes at the awed, uplifted look on that thin, freckled little face.

Georgia had rung her parents and they'd been only too happy to dig out her old bike and bring it over for Jane, who, it appeared, was a natural horsewoman.

'The thing is,' Georgia said to William now, 'I've spoken to her mother. She's a single parent with four kids and there's just no way she can afford a horse for Jane. And she's too proud to let me help. As it is she's embarrassed about the bike and worried that Jane's imposing.'

'I'll bend my mind to it,' William said. 'What plans have you got for Wendell?'

Georgia grimaced. 'None. In fact I'm beginning to wonder whether I shouldn't give Wendell and Connie away... they need to be ridden and...'

'Don't cry,' William said gently after a while.

'I haven't for ages,' she wept, then blew her nose. 'It's just that I don't really know what I'll do; I feel so useless.'

'Georgia—do you blame me for any of this? Is it all tied up in your mind—my going and the accident?'

She didn't pretend to misunderstand, but her eyes widened suddenly because it had not occurred to her before. To blame him, that was. She had only blamed herself—for taking his departure so badly, for not being able to fulfil her promise to him that she wouldn't be devastated, for trying to bury it all beneath so much work. And now that her work had been taken from her, perhaps permanently, now that she felt like a rudderless ship...

Yes, of course it was all tied up in her mind, she acknowledged, but that was not his fault...

She sighed and said huskily, 'No, I don't blame you, Will. And I think I should go to bed now.' She sat up and he didn't resist. 'Thanks for the comfort and kind words. Thanks for the Scrabble. And thanks,' she said with a whimsical little smile, 'for that little display of bad temper this evening. It did my ego a bit of good.'

He didn't attempt to rise as she got up awkwardly and reached for her crutches. He lay back and watched her with his eyes narrowed and his hair lying on his forehead in a way that she loved, then said only, 'Georgia?'

'What, Will?' she whispered.

'It's not impossible, you know. Even with your cast.'

'I don't suppose it is. I...don't feel like it, though. I...I'm sorry.'

'Not at all? Not since I've been here?'

She felt the colour rising in her cheeks and managed to say ruefully, 'I cannot tell a lie, Will—yes, I've thought about it. I suppose it's only natural—I'm still sleeping in the same bed—but it wouldn't be any good. I just know that.

'I think Scheherazade might have gone for ever, you see. And what's left is not the Georgia Newnham you knew and might have been drawn back to. Perhaps she only existed in that small space of time, I don't know, but it's not the same.'

'Do you really think I want an eternal Scheherazade, Georgia?'

'I really think so, Will.'

'What brought this on?'

She paused and wondered what *had* brought it on, and her shoulders slumped suddenly. 'I don't know,' she said barely audibly. 'Remembering the accident, perhaps. I don't know.'

He stood up at last, and when she tensed he said drily, 'Relax; I'm not going to touch you. Only tell you that your appearance means nothing to me and nor does your cast. But...' he paused '...it's become obvious the injury I did you was too great ever to forget, and for that I can only say I'll always be sorry.' He stopped, and his eyes never left her face when he said, 'I promised once not to make things worse for you, Georgia—is that what I'm doing now?'

'How...?'

'By being an eternal reminder of what happened even if you don't blame me.'

She couldn't say anything because she wasn't sure of the truth.

He waited, then his lips twisted and he said, 'It's all right, I think I know now. How will you manage?'

Her lips parted and her heart started to beat unevenly. 'If you go, do you mean?'

'When I go, Georgia,' he said gently, and saw the flare of shock in her eyes but made no move to touch her.

She swallowed. 'My parents will help, I guess. Or find me someone to help. I don't know... But I'll be fine. When...?'

'Tomorrow,' he said very quietly. 'Is there any point in delaying it?'

'No... Oh, no,' she whispered out of a paper-dry throat.

'Promise me one thing.' He took her hand.

'What?' There was a curious roaring in her ears that made both speech and hearing difficult.

'Don't give up.' And he raised her hand to his mouth and kissed her knuckles briefly. 'Goodnight.'

'G-goodnight,' she stammered, and heaven alone knew how, but she stemmed the tide of panic and despair that was rising within her. 'I'll always remember what you did for me.'

He smiled, but it didn't reach his eyes. 'Take care, Georgia.'

'You too, Will!' And she turned away before she broke down and swung herself to the safety of her bedroom.

She slept barely at all, and was tormented by a sense of anguish so great she could barely breathe.

All the time I was fooling myself, she marvelled. All the time I was telling him it was no good, I was hoping against hope. Hoping that he'd stay and battle it out with me, wear me down, make me believe. And now this... This sense of desolation, greater than I've ever known. Greater than the thought that I might never ride again.

What if I go to him now and tell him the plain, simple truth? That I love him as I'll never love anyone else? But the sense of hurt and injury and inadequacy when he left was so great I couldn't see past it, and I still can't believe that he loves me...

What does that change, though? How does that change him? I don't know, I just don't know, nor will I ever know whether his coming back was inspired by pity...

She must have drifted into an uneasy sleep at the crack of dawn, and she woke a couple of hours later with a start, and a sudden resolution in her heart. If nothing else, before William Brady left she would tell him the truth, *her* truth...

But when she got downstairs Jane—who had taken to coming to do the stalls before school as well—was there, Brenda was there and they were both looking sad, which told its own tale.

Georgia clutched the door of the stall Brenda was working in and said unevenly, 'Has he gone?'

'Yes. He called a taxi about half an hour ago. He said to tell you he's left something for you on his desk.'

Georgia closed her eyes. 'Could you—would you mind getting it for me, Brenda?'

'Sure.' She came back within moments with a folder in her hand. 'Photos, by the look of it—oh!'

Photos they were—glossy blow-ups of Brenda at work, of Jane as she sat on Wendell looking exalted. Photos of Connie, of the Davidson kids—her first pupils—but by far the most were of herself.

Photos of her sitting on her stand with her hand imperiously raised to make a point to a pupil, her swinging her crutches with determination, her sitting at her desk in her new office with her chin in her hands, her leaning laughing against a stall door with Wendell nuzzling her shoulder, her standing beside Connie, giving her a carrot, her leaning on a fence as she watched Connie and Wendell playing in the sunlight...

She closed the folder with sudden tears rolling down her cheeks, and only then noticed the writing on it, which said simply, 'My Scheherazade.'

'Why did you let him go, Georgie?' Brenda said softly. 'I thought you were so right for each other and he was such a lovely man.'

'Because I'm a fool, Brenda,' she wept. 'But I'm still not sure if we were right for each other.'

CHAPTER NINE

'DARLING,' her mother said agitatedly only an hour later as she ran up the front steps, 'why did you let him go?'

Georgia grimaced. 'I suppose he rang you. Seeing as I haven't,' she added with a touch of asperity, but not so much towards her mother as herself. As if to say to herself, For heaven's sake don't break down. They've had enough to bear as it is.

'Yes, he rang from the airport— Oh, Georgie!' she gasped as her gaze fell on the photos spread out on the kitchen table. 'They're wonderful! Oh, he's captured the essence of you! The spirit, the determination, the lovely sense of humour—'

'Do you think so?' Georgia said casually. 'He's a man of many talents, our Will.'

'The kind of man,' her mother said with a sudden quiet determination of her own, 'a plaster cast, crutches and everything else can't eliminate. Georgie, please, *tell* me what went wrong. Don't shut me out, my darling child.'

And Georgia stared at her mother then dropped her face into her hands—and told her the whole, plain truth.

'I thought it must have been something like that,' her mother said sadly. 'Oh, it's such a pity. I thought he was so nice!'

'I thought he was nice too,' Georgia said. 'Everyone did. Brenda's devastated,' she added with an attempt at humour. 'So's Jane—'

'Jane!' her mother said. 'I almost forgot. That's the other thing he said, on the phone from the airport.'

Georgia looked bewildered. 'What about Jane?'

'He said why not suggest a formal agreement to her mother? Instead of payment for the work she does, she gets one lesson a week and the use of Wendell to take to the pony club.'

'She might agree to that,' Georgia said thoughtfully—and then broke down completely.

'My dear,' her mother said gently at last, 'are you so sure he doesn't love you?'

'No, I'm not,' Georgia wept. 'I don't know what to think any more—but what would you think? I mean, I couldn't hold him the first time, so why now?'

'He could have changed. It *could* have taken him some time to realise what he felt for you. Georgia, I've learnt a bit more about him myself lately—'

'I can imagine!'

'Nevertheless, did you know that he's quite brilliant? He was brilliant at school, got honours in law *and* arts at university but chose journalism against all opposition because he felt it was the right basis for his writing career. Georgie, sometimes these very clever, intellectual men are not easy to know. I think that's why his mother ran away from Spencer; she might have felt she just wasn't getting through.'

'Who's to say I'd succeed any better with her son than she did with his father?' Georgia asked wearily.

'For one thing you're not her, and for another William is not an exact replica of his father. Georgie—' her mother stared at her helplessly '—he might have changed.'

'I suppose so,' Georgia said miserably. 'But...' She shrugged. 'I'm not renowned for my—wisdom in these matters.'

'And the fact that he's gone again is another mark against him, I suppose,' her mother mused, not troubling to deny Georgia's allegation against herself. 'Well,' she said presently, 'for the moment we'll have to think of a way for you to go along until the cast comes off. You won't be able to manage your lessons on your own. I know!'

'What?' Georgia said listlessly.

But her mother decided to preserve an air of mystery. 'Just you leave it to me, pet! Why don't you go and wash your face and have a little lie-down?'

It was sufficient evidence of Georgia's state of mind that she did. To her regret. Because when she got up her mother triumphantly imparted the news that her cousin Laura was coming to stay with her for two weeks.

She groaned. 'Mum—no!'

'Why not? Neil has tracked down his father, apparently, in the wilds of Tasmania, and would like to spend a little time with him, alone. So she's at a loose end anyway. And she's almost as good with horses as you are. She said she'd be delighted to help out.'

'I can imagine,' Georgia said gloomily. 'I suppose you told her I was William-less, and why?'

'Well, naturally. She had to know.'

'Naturally. I don't know why I don't just go away somewhere,' Georgia said exasperatedly.

'Because you're a fighter, my dear, not a quitter!' her mother said bracingly, causing her daughter to look at her with suspicion.

'What are you plotting, Mum?'

Her mother looked injured. 'Why?'

'I don't know,' Georgia said slowly. 'That didn't sound quite like you, I guess. Mum, you wouldn't do anything to bring us together again, would you? I mean, try to meddle and interfere?'

Her mother, who also had cornflower-blue eyes, opened them very wide. 'I hope I'm not that kind of a person!' she said with dignity.

'I hope so too...'

'Georgie—' this was said firmly '—no, I wouldn't do that. But I am a meddler in some respects. For example, you were starting to look better but now you're looking all haunted again, so I'm going to do something about that. With Laura's help. But in the meantime I'm going to pick her up from the airport. Would you like to come?'

'No, thanks.'

'Well, don't brood too much, darling. I expect you did do the right thing—not to be sure of a man is not a happy situation, although can one ever be entirely sure?'

Georgia stared at her, then smiled reluctantly. 'You must know Dad adores you.'

'Well, I'd like to think so,' her mother said with a sigh. 'But there are times when I fear I'm such a trial to him...'

'No, you're not. Look, off you go before we both get maudlin.'

'I'm gone,' her mother said, then hesitated. 'Will you be all right?'

'Fine. The tears are over, I promise.'

But of course they weren't, not in her heart, not when she was alone in bed at night, and despite the fact that

between them Laura and her mother gave her little time
to brood.

Amongst other things, they cooked up a storm for
her, carted her off to the hairdresser, where she had a
new, shorter, jaunty cut, and to the beautician, where
she had a facial and a manicure, they went right through
her wardrobe, tossing out for charity what they considered old hat, and bullied her into acquiring some new
clothes.

And with rare tact, beyond saying how sorry she was
when they first met, Laura made no mention of William.
Even her uncle Adrian, who came to see them both
several times in those weeks, made no mention of
William Brady.

They were also all there to support her when the cast
finally came off, when she looked with disfavour at her
thin, pale leg but gave a huge sigh of relief at exchanging
her crutches for a walking stick and tried to bend her
mind to getting the leg strong again.

But it happened, on a hot, bright early afternoon, the
day before Laura was to go back to Sydney, that Georgia
found herself thinking, I should have known it was too
good to be true.

'Georgia, there's someone to see you. Let me help you
down; I'll take over the lesson.'

Georgia looked down at Laura from the chair William
had built her and said impatiently, 'Can't they wait? I've
only about ten minutes to go.'

'No, they can't—down you come!'

'But who is it?'

'Georgia Newnham, will you just do as you're told?'
Laura commanded, looking every inch a blonde goddess,
and an irate one at that. 'It's important.'

'It's not...?' Georgia stared down at her with her heart in her mouth.

Laura's expression softened. 'Go and see for yourself.'

It was William.

She gasped and clutched the doorframe.

'Why...what...? I don't understand.'

'Don't you?' he said drily.

'They've been in touch? Laura or...?' Georgia whispered, horrified, then cleared her throat and said in a more normal voice, 'If you *think* I want you back at the behest of my family—'

'No.' He studied her new hairstyle, the clothes she wore that he'd never seen before, and added, 'But I'd like to think that once and for all we could talk things over—more rationally.'

Georgia looked around desperately and he said before she could speak, 'You're right, not here. Will you come away with me for a few days, Georgia?'

'Where? I mean, no. I mean...'

'Then I'll just have to hijack you again,' he said, his lips twisting. 'Laura's packed a bag for you and I came with my own transport. Do I have to carry you down or will you come quietly?'

'You wouldn't!'

'Oh, yes, I would, Georgia,' he said softly but with definite intent.

'But I can't just walk out! Laura's going home tomorrow, and—'

'No, she's not.'

'And it was *your* idea this riding school—what did you say?'

'Laura's not going home tomorrow. Neil's flying up to stay with her here for a week.'

Georgia opened her mouth, closed it, then said faintly, 'How could they?'

He raised a wry eyebrow but said gravely, 'Everyone is of the opinion that you need a few days of rest and relaxation. It's wonderful to see you out of that cast, Georgia,' he added gently.

Sudden tears pricked her eyes, and when he took her hand she didn't resist, although she did say rather challengingly, 'Nothing's changed.'

'Not unless you want it to,' he agreed. 'Let's go.'

'Where are we going?' she said wearily when they were driving away in his car—a very smart, almost brand-new BMW.

'How about Coolum?'

'*Where* at Coolum?'

'The Hyatt. I have a villa there.'

'I might have known,' she said darkly.

'You disapprove?' He glanced at her wryly.

'I can't help thinking back to the time you accused me of having everything handed to me on a platter by a benevolent daddy.'

He grinned briefly. 'The villa wasn't handed to me by my father. I earned most of the money for it with my own hands and the rest came from splitting the proceeds of the Sydney house with my mother. When I said that to you, Georgia, I was accusing you of being a spoilt little rich girl. Something I've changed my mind about entirely, as I thought you knew.'

Georgia sighed and replied laconically, 'I don't know what I know or don't know any more, Will.'

'There's a swimming pool up there,' he said after a time. 'As well as the beach.'

Georgia laid her head back. 'Sounds nice—Will, I hope you don't mind, but I'm feeling unusually out of conversation.'

'Don't mind me,' he murmured.

She didn't.

It took them a little under an hour to reach Coolum once they'd passed through Brisbane. She blinked as he pulled into the driveway of an impressive villa in the Ambassadors' Circle at the Hyatt, Coolum complex, which included a resort hotel, a convention centre and condominiums. There was also a sports centre, restaurants, shops and a magnificent golf course.

The Ambassador villas curved around their own pool, tennis courts and the Regency Club run by the Hyatt, and they faced the golf course. They were the biggest and most prestigious accommodation in the complex— separate houses, in fact—and Georgia would have been impressed, had she been in the mood to be impressed, as William gave her a guided tour of his villa.

The tiled foyer had a beautiful curved staircase leading to the second floor, and the lounge, dining room, study, breakfast room and kitchen were on the ground floor. All the main rooms were luxurious, decorated in lovely pastels and with thick carpeting, beautiful paintings, lamps and furniture. Upstairs there were three bedrooms with *en-suite* bathrooms and on the flat roof a wooden deck and a spa.

'Very nice,' she said neutrally as she came carefully down from the roof. 'I'll have my own bedroom, Will.'

'Take your choice,' he invited, and picked up her bag. 'Can I make a suggestion? Why don't you come for a swim in the pool?'

'I don't know if—' Georgia began.

'Laura packed a swimsuit for you. I'll meet you up there,' he said, and turned away.

Georgia sat on the bed and studied her hands for a good five minutes. Then she flicked open the bag that her treacherous cousin Laura had not only packed for her but had also led her into buying the contents of, for just this occasion. She examined those contents article by article.

There was a pair of white linen trousers and a matching blouse with padded shoulders and heavy lace inserts. There was a gold belt to go with it and flat gold shoes, a lovely long skirt in a soft plum colour with a matching waistcoat-style top and an interchangeable pale gold overblouse with long sleeves.

There were two pairs of shorts and tops, a slip dress with a long skirt and shoestring straps, to be worn alone or with a tiny ribbed T-shirt beneath, and a pair of linen and raffia sandals. And her new navy blue cotton knit swimsuit with little white flowers on it and a matching voluminous cotton shirt to go over it.

All her new underwear was there, and—her hands stilled as she took it out last—the dream nightgown that both Laura and her mother had virtually bullied her into buying. It was in the finest buttercup satin, with blonde lace edging the deep V neckline. Everything was brand-new and had never been worn before.

Were they planning this all along? she wondered. When they were coercing me into shops and boutiques, getting me manicured and massaged and all the rest? Probably. How did they prevail upon William to go along with it? I just can't bear the thought of them telling him I was devastated for a second time...

* * *

He was the only person at the pool as it sparkled invitingly in its quiet, leafy surroundings, with Mount Coolum in the background. He was lying on a lounger, wearing only a pair of dark red board shorts, his body as beautiful as ever but well tanned now.

She looked away and laid her walking stick down on the lounger next to him, took her blouse off and stepped straight into the pool. It was heavenly, and she floated on her back and concentrated on all the things she could do now and how she was to start physiotherapy next week, as well as exercising in a pool...

'Nice?'

She looked around to see that he had stepped in and was floating beside her. 'Lovely.'

'You must feel incredibly free.'

'I do. I—I was just thinking about it.'

'Did you feel lopsided when it came off?'

'Incredibly. I still do at times, so if I fall over you'll know why.'

'I'll watch out. The sun's starting to set.'

'Does that mean anything in particular?' she queried.

'I just thought,' he said idly, 'you might like to go in and change soon, then we could have a drink on the terrace before I take you out to dinner.'

'Not cooking tonight, Will?' she said flippantly.

'I can, if you'd prefer. I thought you might enjoy getting out and about for a change.'

'I would,' she said hastily, but not because she particularly wanted to, rather to avoid spending an evening alone with him in the villa.

Unfortunately, as she looked into his hazel eyes beneath his sleek wet hair she detected a little glint that told her he knew exactly what was going through her mind. Which had the effect of stiffening her resolve, and she stared back defiantly.

But he only smiled faintly and murmured, 'Let's go.'

And it was while she was dressing that she stopped to wonder what her resolve in the matter was...

He met her at the bottom of the stairs.

He had changed into grey trousers and a crisp, long-sleeved white shirt, open at the throat, and had a navy blazer over his arm. He was more formally dressed than she'd ever seen him, and she stopped on the second last step because, privately, he took her breath away for a moment.

He also studied her comprehensively, from her sleek, shining hair, cut to curve just under her chin now, and the delicate make-up she wore to the austere lines of the straight blouse over her plum skirt that were offset by the lovely fine pale gold silk and the little metal mesh bag she carried. And he smiled at her as he held out his hand and said, 'You look stunning, Miss Newnham.'

She cleared her throat, didn't take his hand because she was afraid of touching him, and said quietly, 'You look rather good yourself, Will. I must say it is nice to get dressed up again. Did you mention something about a drink?'

The stars had started to prick the darkening sky as they sat on the terrace and she sipped a long, cool drink while he had a beer. The golf course lay before them and the perfume of mown grass wafted on the faint breeze. There was a lake reflecting the last of the sunset not far away, and that was how the conversation got going.

'See that water?' he said idly. 'It's a bit of a nemesis for me.'

'Oh? Why?'

'I keep losing golf balls in it.'

'So it's a water hazard on the course—I didn't know you played golf, Will. What's your handicap?'

'Six. On my good days,' he said lightly.

'I might have known—but you can't lose that many balls and be a six.'

'Enough—and what might you have known, Georgia?'

She shrugged. 'That you'd be good at it.'

'There are some things I'm not good at at all,' he said after a pause.

Georgia sipped her drink and said before she could stop herself, 'All the same, brilliant at school, honours in both law and arts at university—a right intellectual, I'm told!'

'Who by?'

She grimaced. 'My mother. She thought you were so nice—by the way, your suggestion about Jane has worked,' she said, hoping to switch the conversation adroitly. 'She went to her first pony club meet on Wendell last week.'

'I'm glad. How's Brenda?'

'Still missing you. Thank you for those photos.'

'My pleasure.'

Georgia took another sip of her drink, then said in an oddly strangled sort of voice, 'I can't do this, Will.' And she went to get up but he reached over and put a restraining hand on her wrist.

'Do what?' he said barely audibly as she subsided.

'Make trivial conversation with you,' she replied bitterly.

'Then let's talk about us.'

'I can't do that either—tell me something. Who got in touch with you? Laura? That's my bet, Will.' And her eyes were filled with angry irony.

'It was the other way around, Georgia.'

'But you said...' she objected tautly, and then paused. 'You implied, anyway, that—'

'That they were happy to connive with me? They were. You see, I called them all together for a round-table conference.'

'What?' she gasped.

'It occurred to me that I might as well enlist your family again, Georgia,' he said, and instead of imprisoning her by her wrist ran his fingers lightly along the inside of it. 'And they agreed that if I was going to make one last stand with you I should wait until your cast came off, because it was obviously an impediment to how you saw yourself.'

His hazel gaze captured hers and she couldn't help the faint tinge of colour that rose to her cheeks. 'We also agreed I'd be better to take you by surprise.' he added.

'I don't believe it,' she whispered.

'Why don't you check with your mother—would she lie to you?'

'No...' Georgia looked dazed, and then said with an effort, 'So what made you change your mind?'

'The hope that I might have been wrong,' he said, very quietly.

'What about?'

'You said you didn't blame me for what happened to you. I didn't believe you, and I thought at the time that I would always be a reminder of it, as I told you. It seemed to fit in with you being so sure things could never be the same between us. When I looked back, though, I thought of other things, and that led me to hope...hope that I hadn't killed everything you felt stone-dead by leaving you the way I did. The first time.'

Georgia swallowed and listened to some sleepy birds settling finally in a nearby clump of trees. 'Did you really ever believe that, Will?' she said huskily and bleakly at last. 'I rather thought I gave myself away completely.'

'Not when you wept for yourself, Georgia. You seemed quite resolved and withdrawn afterwards. That's why I went. *Was* I wrong?'

'Will...' She took an uncertain breath as her mind whirled, and said unevenly, 'The thing I've never been able to resolve is why you came back.'

'Could that be because you've never been prepared to listen to me or believe me or—? I was going to say trust me, but perhaps that's asking a bit much. But you have *never* wanted to listen, Georgia,' he said intently.

'I know. I...' she whispered, but couldn't go on.

'Could I tell you now?'

She could only nod.

'It's actually quite simple,' he said a little drily. 'Although, at the time, it seemed a lot more complicated. I left you the first time because I told myself all the things I told you, or—' a faint smile touched his mouth '—some of the things you wrested out of me. That I was cynical because of my parents, that I was a loner, that I just wasn't made to be tied down, not built for it, et cetera, et cetera, and had one unfortunate experience behind me to prove it.

'I told myself we were such opposites it could only end in disaster, that our almost instant attraction *was* because I'd grown tired of meaningless encounters and it had been some time since I'd come out of my ivory tower.'

Georgia made a strange little sound but he stilled it with a suddenly firmer pressure on her wrist.

'I told myself you needed a different kind of man, not the kind of fringe-dweller I seemed to have become,' he went on with self-directed irony. 'I foolishly saw myself as the intellectual you accused me of being earlier and you as someone more earthy, who needed a more down-to-earth man than I was, to give you all the children you wanted and cope with all your energy and your good works.

'I told myself all these things again and again, through the horror of Bosnia, the isolation of the Falklands, the torment of being on an island that bore your name. And the torment,' he said very quietly, 'of imagining you with another man.'

'Go on,' Georgia whispered.

'Then I read something somewhere—a quote from a poem that went "whoever loved, that loved not at first sight?". And the simple truth hit me—that for the first time I'd fallen in *love*. That you were in my heart and my blood and all our differences made not one bit of difference to the fact that you were the only woman I was bitterly unhappy without, the only woman it mattered if I couldn't have. That I would willingly give you ten children and all the horses in the world if you would only take me to your bed and keep me there with your own, special brand of magic.'

'Will...' she said, battling for breath. 'Oh, I don't know what to say. I still...' She shook her head dazedly.

'Let me finish, then,' he said gently. 'What I wasn't prepared for when I came back to tell you all this was the havoc I myself had wreaked. And I didn't know you blamed me for the accident then either,' he said.

'I *didn't*. I blamed myself.'

'Georgia,' he said, and his eyes were grim and direct in the light coming out from the lounge, 'can you ever forgive me?'

'Will,' she said tremulously, 'I—'

'For letting you down and letting you go in a way that made you think I cared nothing for you? For turning my back on something so special between us that it almost broke your heart?' And there was something in his eyes that was devastatingly intent and questioning as he went on, 'For making it so that you couldn't believe me, couldn't believe the easy-to-say words, the intimate moments, could only believe it was pity and hated it so much—'

'Yes,' she breathed, distraught. 'Plus I felt so—such a wreck—'

'Do you know something, Georgia? If I thought I'd loved you before, it was nothing to how much I loved you when you were battling with those crutches, when you were tired and thin, with all your dreams in doubt, but still going on...'

'Why did you leave again, then, Will?' she said hoarsely.

He sighed and laid his head back. 'I've told you the first reason. The second was much more—down-to-earth, if you like. I wanted you so badly. I couldn't stand being knocked back and having to go on living in the same house with you.'

Georgia's lips parted and her eyes widened. 'Will?' she said. 'Even with the cast on?'

His lips twisted. 'I'm afraid so. I guess you'd be entitled to say, "That's so like a man," but—'

'Will,' Georgia broke in with sudden urgency, 'if I sounded resolved and withdrawn that night, it was to do with this—I love you, I never stopped, but I couldn't believe you loved me; I couldn't...believe it. I was going to tell you the morning you left but you'd gone,' she said with tears in her eyes.

'Has anything I've said tonight changed your mind, Georgia?'

She stared at him and noticed for the first time that he looked drawn and tired, but it was there again, that something in his eyes, the expression she'd been unable to read, and her heart leapt suddenly, because now she could read that intimate enquiry between a man and a woman, and knew that it *had* been her perception of herself that had been blocking and impeding her understanding.

She swallowed and said, 'Not you, Will—whoever the poet is that you quoted.'

'Georgia—'

'Plus the things you said about breaking my heart, Will. I didn't think you knew or understood how special things had been—'

'Georgia...' He was on his feet, helping her to rise, then taking her in his arms. 'I love you.'

'This was not my idea,' she said a little later, coming to him in her beautiful buttercup satin nightgown.

He drew his fingers down the V at the front and looked into her eyes. 'No?'

'No. My mother and Laura positively bullied me into buying it.'

A faint smile twisted his lips. 'They did well.'

She took a breath. 'It also hides my leg, Will. I'm a bit embarrassed about it at the moment.'

'That's a pity,' he said very quietly, 'because I'm not in the slightest—I thought I'd put all those fears to rest, my darling.' And he smiled into her eyes, this time his sunlight-after-rain smile.

'Oh,' she said on a breath, 'you really are awfully nice, Will.'

'Not always.' He slid his arms about her waist. 'Don't forget how intractable I become when I can't have you.'

A smile trembled on her lips. 'I have to tell you I love the sound of that.'

'All the same, should we take steps to avoid it?'

'Why not?' she whispered.

'We never did get to eat,' she said drowsily later, lying uncovered beside him with her buttercup nightgown in a heap on the floor.

'No, my Scheherazade, we didn't,' he murmured, and drew his hand down her body.

'So it is still the same for you, Will?'

'It's better. Not only because you've lost none of your skill and your magic but also because now you're mine. Do you remember the first time we did this?'

'Of course. How could I forget? I also remember the first time you kissed me.'

He grinned. 'I should have known then that this was going to become a lifetime hazard for me.'

'Hazard?' She raised an eyebrow at him.

He kissed her lingeringly, then said, 'Mmm—this inability I have to keep my hands off you. I don't usually go around kissing girls like that.'

She laughed softly. '*I* should have known—and I think I did have some intimation of it—what a perfectly *perfect* stranger you were to become.'

'I have to say I like the sound of that, and in view...' He paused, playing with her breasts this time, cupping, plucking and finally kissing each nipple in turn. 'In view of all these matters, will you marry me, Georgia?'

'Yes, please—oh, yes, Will. Should we do it—? No,' she said with a little sigh.

'Do what?'

'I was going to suggest we went away and did it by ourselves, but that would be such a disappointment to them all.'

He groaned, then laughed. 'You're right; we won't disappoint them. So long as we don't have to wait too long.'

'Will,' she said presently, her breathing ragged and her heart beating rapidly with desire, 'I asked you this once before, but—could we do it again?'

'Georgia,' he said, drawing her hips to his and seeking the satiny hollow at the base of her throat with his lips, 'I thought you'd never ask.'

MILLS & BOON®

Next Month's Romances

♡

Each month you can choose from a wide variety of romance novels from Mills & Boon. Below are the new titles to look out for next month from the Presents and Enchanted series.

Presents™

MISTAKEN FOR A MISTRESS	Jacqueline Baird
NIGHT OF SHAME	Miranda Lee
THE GUILTY WIFE	Sally Wentworth
LOOKING AFTER DAD	Elizabeth Oldfield
LOVERS' LIES	Daphne Clair
CLOSE RELATIONS	Lynsey Stevens
THE SEDUCTION TRAP	Sara Wood
HER PERSONAL BODYGUARD	Susan Mc Carthy

Enchanted™

THE DAUGHTER OF THE MANOR	Betty Neels
A BUSINESS ENGAGEMENT	Jessica Steele
RUNAWAY HONEYMOON	Ruth Jean Dale
McALLISTER'S BABY	Trisha David
BRIDE ON THE RANCH	Barbara McMahon
AMBER AND THE SHEIKH	Stephanie Howard
ONCE A COWBOY...	Day Leclaire
PRINCE OF DELIGHTS	Renee Roszel

SANDRA BROWN

New York Times bestselling author

HONOUR BOUND

Theirs was an impossible love

"One of fiction's brightest stars!"
—Dallas Morning News

Lucas Greywolf was Aislinn's forbidden
fantasy—and every moment of their
mad dash across Arizona drew her
closer to this unyielding man.

AVAILABLE IN PAPERBACK
FROM MARCH 1997

FREE!

FOUR FREE
specially selected
Presents™ novels
PLUS a FREE Mystery Gift
when you return this page...

Return this coupon and we'll send you 4 Mills & Boon® Presents™ novels and a mystery gift absolutely FREE! We'll even pay the postage and packing for you.

We're making you this offer to introduce you to the benefits of the Reader Service™– FREE home delivery of brand-new Mills & Boon Presents novels, at least a month before they are available in the shops, FREE gifts and a monthly Newsletter packed with information, competitions, author profiles and lots more...

Accepting these FREE books and gift places you under no obligation to buy, you may cancel at any time, even after receiving just your free shipment. Simply complete the coupon below and send it to:

MILLS & BOON READER SERVICE, FREEPOST, CROYDON, SURREY, CR9 3WZ.

READERS IN EIRE PLEASE SEND COUPON TO PO BOX 4546, DUBLIN 24

NO STAMP NEEDED

Yes, please send me 4 free Presents novels and a mystery gift. I understand that unless you hear from me, I will receive 6 superb new titles every month for just £2.20* each, postage and packing free. I am under no obligation to purchase any books and I may cancel or suspend my subscription at any time, but the free books and gift will be mine to keep in any case. (I am over 18 years of age)

P7XE

Ms/Mrs/Miss/Mr _____
BLOCK CAPS PLEASE

Address_____

_____

_____

_____ Postcode _____

RACHEL LEE

◆

A FATEFUL CHOICE

**She arranged her own death—
then changed her mind**

*"Ms Lee's talents as a writer are
dazzling. Put this author's name on
your list of favourites right now!"*
—Romantic Times

AVAILABLE IN PAPERBACK
FROM MARCH 1997